The Swoop!
Or, How Clarence Saved England
A Tale of the Great Invasion

&

A Man of Means

P. G. Wodehouse

The Swoop! or, How Clarence Saved England: A Tale of the Great Invasion
&
A Man of Means

ISBN: 978-1-64799-294-1

CONTENTS

THE SWOOP!
Or How Clarence Saved England

PREFACE

It may be thought by some that in the pages which follow I have painted in too lurid colours the horrors of a foreign invasion of England. Realism in art, it may be argued, can be carried too far. I prefer to think that the majority of my readers will acquit me of a desire to be unduly sensational. It is necessary that England should be roused to a sense of her peril, and only by setting down without flinching the probable results of an invasion can this be done. This story, I may mention, has been written and published purely from a feeling of patriotism and duty. Mr. Alston Rivers' sensitive soul will be jarred to its foundations if it is a financial success. So will mine. But in a time of national danger we feel that the risk must be taken. After all, at the worst, it is a small sacrifice to make for our country.

P. G. WODEHOUSE

THE SWOOP!

Or How Clarence Saved England

PART ONE

CHAPTER 1

AN ENGLISH BOY'S HOME

August the First, 19—

Clarence Chugwater looked around him with a frown, and gritted his teeth.

"England—my England!" he moaned.

Clarence was a sturdy lad of some fourteen summers. He was neatly, but not gaudily, dressed in a flat-brimmed hat, a coloured handkerchief, a flannel shirt, a bunch of ribbons, a haversack, football shorts, brown boots, a whistle, and a hockey-stick. He was, in fact, one of General Baden-Powell's Boy Scouts.

Scan him closely. Do not dismiss him with a passing glance; for you are looking at the Boy of Destiny, at Clarence MacAndrew Chugwater, who saved England.

To-day those features are familiar to all. Everyone has seen the Chugwater Column in Aldwych, the equestrian statue in Chugwater Road (formerly Piccadilly), and the picture-postcards in the stationers' windows. That bulging forehead, distended with useful information; that massive chin; those eyes, gleaming behind their spectacles; that tout ensemble; that je ne sais quoi.

In a word, Clarence!

He could do everything that the Boy Scout must learn to do. He could low like a bull. He could gurgle like a wood-pigeon. He could imitate the cry of the turnip in order to deceive rabbits. He could smile and whistle simultaneously in accordance with Rule 8 (and only those who have tried this know how difficult it is). He could spoor, fell trees, tell the character from the boot-sole, and fling the squaler. He did all these things well, but what he was really best at was flinging the squaler.

Clarence, on this sultry August afternoon, was tensely occupied tracking the family cat across the dining-room carpet by its foot-prints. Glancing up for a moment, he caught sight of the other members of the family.

"England, my England!" he moaned.

It was indeed a sight to extract tears of blood from any Boy Scout. The table had been moved back against the wall, and in the cleared space Mr. Chugwater, whose duty it was to have set an example to his children, was playing diabolo. Beside him, engrossed in cup-and-ball, was his wife. Reggie Chugwater, the eldest son, the heir, the hope of the house, was reading the cricket news in an early edition of the evening paper. Horace, his brother, was playing pop-in-taw with his sister Grace and Grace's fiance, Ralph Peabody. Alice, the other Miss Chugwater, was mending a Badminton racquet.

Not a single member of that family was practising with the rifle, or drilling, or learning to make bandages.

Clarence groaned.

"If you can't play without snorting like that, my boy," said Mr. Chugwater, a little irritably, "you must find some other game. You made me jump just as I was going to beat my record."

"Talking of records," said Reggie, "Fry's on his way to his eighth successive century. If he goes on like this, Lancashire will win the championship."

"I thought he was playing for Somerset," said Horace.

"That was a fortnight ago. You ought to keep up to date in an important subject like cricket."

Once more Clarence snorted bitterly.

"I'm sure you ought not to be down on the floor, Clarence," said Mr. Chugwater anxiously. "It is so draughty, and you have evidently got a nasty cold. Must you lie on the floor?"

"I am spooring," said Clarence with simple dignity.

"But I'm sure you can spoor better sitting on a chair with a nice book."

2

"I think the kid's sickening for something," put in Horace critically. "He's deuced roopy. What's up, Clarry?"

"I was thinking," said Clarence, "of my country—of England."

"What's the matter with England?"

"She's all right," murmured Ralph Peabody.

"My fallen country!" sighed Clarence, a not unmanly tear bedewing the glasses of his spectacles. "My fallen, stricken country!"

"That kid," said Reggie, laying down his paper, "is talking right through his hat. My dear old son, are you aware that England has never been so strong all round as she is now? Do you ever read the papers? Don't you know that we've got the Ashes and the Golf Championship, and the Wibbley-wob Championship, and the Spiropole, Spillikins, Puff-Feather, and Animal Grab Championships? Has it come to your notice that our croquet pair beat America last Thursday by eight hoops? Did you happen to hear that we won the Hop-skip-and-jump at the last Olympic Games? You've been out in the woods, old sport."

Clarence's heart was too full for words. He rose in silence, and quitted the room.

"Got the pip or something!" said Reggie. "Rum kid! I say, Hirst's bowling well! Five for twenty-three so far!"

Clarence wandered moodily out of the house. The Chugwaters lived in a desirable villa residence, which Mr. Chugwater had built in Essex. It was a typical Englishman's Home. Its name was Nasturtium Villa.

As Clarence walked down the road, the excited voice of a newspaper-boy came to him. Presently the boy turned the corner, shouting, "Ker-lapse of Surrey! Sensational bowling at the Oval!"

He stopped on seeing Clarence.

"Paper, General?"

Clarence shook his head. Then he uttered a startled exclamation, for his eye had fallen on the poster.

It ran as follows:—

SURREY
DOING
BADLY
GERMAN ARMY LANDS IN ENGLAND

CHAPTER 2

THE INVADERS

Clarence flung the boy a halfpenny, tore a paper from his grasp, and scanned it eagerly. There was nothing to interest him in the body of the journal, but he found what he was looking for in the stop-press space. "Stop press news," said the paper. "Fry not out, 104. Surrey 147 for 8. A German army landed in Essex this afternoon. Loamshire Handicap: Spring Chicken, 1; Salome, 2; Yip-i-addy, 3. Seven ran."

Essex! Then at any moment the foe might be at their doors; more, inside their doors. With a passionate cry, Clarence tore back to the house.

He entered the dining-room with the speed of a highly-trained Marathon winner, just in time once more to prevent Mr. Chugwater lowering his record.

"The Germans!" shouted Clarence. "We are invaded!"

This time Mr. Chugwater was really annoyed.

"If I have told you once about your detestable habit of shouting in the house, Clarence, I have told you a hundred times. If you cannot be a Boy Scout quietly, you must stop being one altogether. I had got up to six that time."

"But, father——"

"Silence! You will go to bed this minute; and I shall consider the question whether you are to have any supper. It will depend largely on your behaviour between now and then. Go!"

"But, father——"

Clarence dropped the paper, shaken with emotion. Mr. Chugwater's sternness deepened visibly.

"Clarence! Must I speak again?"

He stooped and removed his right slipper.

Clarence withdrew.

Reggie picked up the paper.

"That kid," he announced judicially, "is off his nut! Hullo! I told you so! Fry not out, 104. Good old Charles!"

4

"I say," exclaimed Horace, who sat nearest the window, "there are two rummy-looking chaps coming to the front door, wearing a sort of fancy dress!"

"It must be the Germans," said Reggie. "The paper says they landed here this afternoon. I expect——"

A thunderous knock rang through the house. The family looked at one another. Voices were heard in the hall, and next moment the door opened and the servant announced "Mr. Prinsotto and Mr. Aydycong."

"Or, rather," said the first of the two newcomers, a tall, bearded, soldierly man, in perfect English, "Prince Otto of Saxe-Pfennig and Captain the Graf von Poppenheim, his aide-de-camp."

"Just so—just so!" said Mr. Chugwater, affably. "Sit down, won't you?"

The visitors seated themselves. There was an awkward silence.

"Warm day!" said Mr. Chugwater.

"Very!" said the Prince, a little constrainedly.

"Perhaps a cup of tea? Have you come far?"

"Well—er—pretty far. That is to say, a certain distance. In fact, from Germany."

"I spent my summer holiday last year at Dresden. Capital place!"

"Just so. The fact is, Mr.—er—"

"Chugwater. By the way—my wife, Mrs. Chugwater."

The prince bowed. So did his aide-de-camp.

"The fact is, Mr. Jugwater," resumed the prince, "we are not here on a holiday."

"Quite so, quite so. Business before pleasure."

The prince pulled at his moustache. So did his aide-de-camp, who seemed to be a man of but little initiative and conversational resource.

"We are invaders."

"Not at all, not at all," protested Mr. Chugwater.

"I must warn you that you will resist at your peril. You wear no uniform—"

"Wouldn't dream of such a thing. Except at the lodge, of course."

"You will be sorely tempted, no doubt. Do not think that I do not appreciate your feelings. This is an Englishman's Home."

Mr. Chugwater tapped him confidentially on the knee.

"And an uncommonly snug little place, too," he said. "Now, if you will forgive me for talking business, you, I gather, propose making some stay in this country."

5

The prince laughed shortly. So did his aide-de-camp. "Exactly," continued Mr. Chugwater, "exactly. Then you will want some pied-a-terre, if you follow me. I shall be delighted to let you this house on remarkably easy terms for as long as you please. Just come along into my study for a moment. We can talk it over quietly there. You see, dealing direct with me, you would escape the middleman's charges, and—"

Gently but firmly he edged the prince out of the room and down the passage.

The aide-de-camp continued to sit staring woodenly at the carpet. Reggie closed quietly in on him.

"Excuse me," he said; "talking shop and all that. But I'm an agent for the Come One Come All Accident and Life Assurance Office. You have heard of it probably? We can offer you really exceptional terms. You must not miss a chance of this sort. Now here's a prospectus—"

Horace sidled forward.

"I don't know if you happen to be a cyclist, Captain—er—Graf; but if you'd like a practically new motorbike, only been used since last November, I can let you—"

There was a swish of skirts as Grace and Alice advanced on the visitor.

"I'm sure," said Grace winningly, "that you're fond of the theatre, Captain Poppenheim. We are getting up a performance of 'Ici on parle Francais,' in aid of the fund for Supplying Square Meals to Old-Age Pensioners. Such a deserving object, you know. Now, how many tickets will you take?"

"You can sell them to your friends, you know," added Mrs. Chugwater.

The aide-de-camp gulped convulsively.

Ten minutes later two penniless men groped their way, dazed, to the garden gate.

"At last," said Prince Otto brokenly, for it was he, "at last I begin to realise the horrors of an invasion—for the invaders."

And together the two men staggered on.

6

CHAPTER 3

ENGLAND'S PERIL

When the papers arrived next morning, it was seen that the situation was even worse than had at first been suspected. Not only had the Germans effected a landing in Essex, but, in addition, no fewer than eight other hostile armies had, by some remarkable coincidence, hit on that identical moment for launching their long-prepared blow.

England was not merely beneath the heel of the invader. It was beneath the heels of nine invaders.

There was barely standing-room.

Full details were given in the Press. It seemed that while Germany was landing in Essex, a strong force of Russians, under the Grand Duke Vodkakoff, had occupied Yarmouth. Simultaneously the Mad Mullah had captured Portsmouth; while the Swiss navy had bombarded Lyme Regis, and landed troops immediately to westward of the bathing-machines. At precisely the same moment China, at last awakened, had swooped down upon that picturesque little Welsh watering-place, Lllgxtplll, and, despite desperate resistance on the part of an excursion of Evanses and Joneses from Cardiff, had obtained a secure foothold. While these things were happening in Wales, the army of Monaco had descended on Auchtermuchty, on the Firth of Clyde. Within two minutes of this disaster, by Greenwich time, a boisterous band of Young Turks had seized Scarborough. And, at Brighton and Margate respectively, small but determined armies, the one of Moroccan brigands, under Raisuli, the other of dark-skinned warriors from the distant isle of Bollygolla, had made good their footing.

This was a very serious state of things.

Correspondents of the Daily Mail at the various points of attack had wired such particulars as they were able. The preliminary parley at Lllgxtplll between Prince Ping Pong Pang, the Chinese general, and Llewellyn Evans, the leader of the Cardiff

7

excursionists, seems to have been impressive to a degree. The former had spoken throughout in pure Chinese, the latter replying in rich Welsh, and the general effect, wired the correspondent, was almost painfully exhilarating.

So sudden had been the attacks that in very few instances was there any real resistance. The nearest approach to it appears to have been seen at Margate.

At the time of the arrival of the black warriors which, like the other onslaughts, took place between one and two o'clock on the afternoon of August Bank Holiday, the sands were covered with happy revellers. When the war canoes approached the beach, the excursionists seem to have mistaken their occupants at first for a troupe of nigger minstrels on an unusually magnificent scale; and it was freely noised abroad in the crowd that they were being presented by Charles Frohmann, who was endeavouring to revive the ancient glories of the Christy Minstrels. Too soon, however, it was perceived that these were no harmless Moore and Burgesses. Suspicion was aroused by the absence of banjoes and tambourines; and when the foremost of the negroes dexterously scalped a small boy, suspicion became certainty.

In this crisis the trippers of Margate behaved well. The Mounted Infantry, on donkeys, headed by Uncle Bones, did much execution. The Ladies' Tormentor Brigade harassed the enemy's flank, and a hastily-formed band of sharp-shooters, armed with three-shies-a-penny balls and milky cocos, undoubtedly troubled the advance guard considerably. But superior force told. After half an hour's fighting the excursionists fled, leaving the beach to the foe.

At Auchtermuchty and Portsmouth no obstacle, apparently, was offered to the invaders. At Brighton the enemy were permitted to land unharmed. Scarborough, taken utterly aback by the boyish vigour of the Young Turks, was an easy prey; and at Yarmouth, though the Grand Duke received a nasty slap in the face from a dexterously-thrown bloater, the resistance appears to have been equally futile.

By tea-time on August the First, nine strongly-equipped forces were firmly established on British soil.

8

CHAPTER 4

WHAT ENGLAND THOUGHT OF IT

Such a state of affairs, disturbing enough in itself, was rendered still more disquieting by the fact that, except for the Boy Scouts, England's military strength at this time was practically nil.

The abolition of the regular army had been the first step. Several causes had contributed to this. In the first place, the Socialists had condemned the army system as unsocial. Privates, they pointed out, were forbidden to hob-nob with colonels, though the difference in their positions was due to a mere accident of birth. They demanded that every man in the army should be a general. Comrade Quelch, in an eloquent speech at Newington Butts, had pointed, amidst enthusiasm, to the republics of South America, where the system worked admirably.

Scotland, too, disapproved of the army, because it was professional. Mr. Smith wrote several trenchant letters to Mr. C. J. B. Marriott on the subject.

So the army was abolished, and the land defence of the country entrusted entirely to the Territorials, the Legion of Frontiersmen, and the Boy Scouts.

But first the Territorials dropped out. The strain of being referred to on the music-hall stage as Teddy-boys was too much for them.

Then the Frontiersmen were disbanded. They had promised well at the start, but they had never been themselves since La Milo had been attacked by the Manchester Watch Committee. It had taken all the heart out of them.

So that in the end England's defenders were narrowed down to the Boy Scouts, of whom Clarence Chugwater was the pride, and a large civilian population, prepared, at any moment, to turn out for their country's sake and wave flags. A certain section of these, too, could sing patriotic songs.

It was inevitable, in the height of the Silly Season, that such a topic as the simultaneous invasion of Great Britain by nine foreign powers should be seized upon by the press. Countless letters poured into the offices of the London daily papers every morning. Space forbids more than the gist of a few of these.

Miss Charlesworth wrote:—"In this crisis I see no alternative. I shall disappear."

Mr. Horatio Bottomley, in John Bull, said that there was some very dirty and underhand work going on, and that the secret history of the invasion would be published shortly. He himself, however, preferred any invader, even the King of Bollygolla, to some K.C.'s he could name, though he was fond of dear old Muir. He wanted to know why Inspector Drew had retired.

The Daily Express, in a thoughtful leader, said that Free Trade evidently meant invaders for all.

Mr. Herbert Gladstone, writing to the Times, pointed out that he had let so many undesirable aliens into the country that he did not see that a few more made much difference.

Mr. George R. Sims made eighteen puns on the names of the invading generals in the course of one number of "Mustard and Cress."

Mr. H. G. Pelissier urged the public to look on the bright side. There was a sun still shining in the sky. Besides, who knew that some foreign marksman might not pot the censor?

Mr. Robert FitzSimmons offered to take on any of the invading generals, or all of them, and if he didn't beat them it would only be because the referee had a wife and seven small children and had asked him as a personal favour to let himself be knocked out. He had lost several fights that way.

The directors of the Crystal Palace wrote a circular letter to the shareholders, pointing out that there was a good time coming. With this addition to the public, the Palace stood a sporting chance of once more finding itself full.

Judge Willis asked: "What is an invasion?"

Signor Scotti cabled anxiously from America (prepaid): "Stands Scotland where it did?"

Mr. Lewis Waller wrote heroically: "How many of them are there? I am usually good for about half a dozen. Are they assassins? I can tackle any number of assassins."

Mr. Seymour Hicks said he hoped they would not hurt George Edwardes.

Mr. George Edwardes said that if they injured Seymour Hicks in any way he would never smile again.

A writer in Answers pointed out that, if all the invaders in the country were piled in a heap, they would reach some of the way to the moon.

Far-seeing men took a gloomy view of the situation. They laid stress on the fact that this counter-attraction was bound to hit first-class cricket hard. For some years gates had shown a tendency to fall off, owing to the growing popularity of golf, tennis, and other games. The desire to see the invaders as they marched through the country must draw away thousands who otherwise would have paid their sixpences at the turnstiles. It was suggested that representations should be made to the invading generals with a view to inducing them to make a small charge to sightseers.

In sporting circles the chief interest centered on the race to London. The papers showed the positions of the various armies each morning in their Runners and Betting columns; six to four on the Germans was freely offered, but found no takers.

Considerable interest was displayed in the probable behaviour of the nine armies when they met. The situation was a curious outcome of the modern custom of striking a deadly blow before actually declaring war. Until the moment when the enemy were at her doors, England had imagined that she was on terms of the most satisfactory friendship with her neighbours. The foe had taken full advantage of this, and also of the fact that, owing to a fit of absent-mindedness on the part of the Government, England had no ships afloat which were not entirely obsolete. Interviewed on the subject by representatives of the daily papers, the Government handsomely admitted that it was perhaps in some ways a silly thing to have done; but, they urged, you could not think of everything. Besides, they were on the point of laying down a Dreadnought, which would be ready in a very few years. Meanwhile, the best thing the public could do was to sleep quietly in their beds. It was Fisher's tip; and Fisher was a smart man.

And all the while the Invaders' Marathon continued.

Who would be the first to reach London?

CHAPTER 5

THE GERMANS REACH LONDON

The Germans had got off smartly from the mark and were fully justifying the long odds laid upon them. That master-strategist, Prince Otto of Saxe-Pfennig, realising that if he wished to reach the Metropolis quickly he must not go by train, had resolved almost at once to walk. Though hampered considerably by crowds of rustics who gathered, gaping, at every point in the line of march, he had made good progress. The German troops had strict orders to reply to no questions, with the result that little time was lost in idle chatter, and in a couple of days it was seen that the army of the Fatherland was bound, barring accidents, to win comfortably.

The progress of the other forces was slower. The Chinese especially had undergone great privations, having lost their way near Llanfairpwlgwnngogogoch, and having been unable to understand the voluble directions given to them by the various shepherds they encountered. It was not for nearly a week that they contrived to reach Chester, where, catching a cheap excursion, they arrived in the metropolis, hungry and footsore, four days after the last of their rivals had taken up their station.

The German advance halted on the wooded heights of Tottenham. Here a camp was pitched and trenches dug.

The march had shown how terrible invasion must of necessity be. With no wish to be ruthless, the troops of Prince Otto had done grievous damage. Cricket-pitches had been trampled down, and in many cases even golf-greens dented by the iron heel of the invader, who rarely, if ever, replaced the divot. Everywhere they had left ruin and misery in their train.

With the other armies it was the same story. Through carefully-preserved woods they had marched, frightening the birds and driving keepers into fits of nervous prostration. Fishing, owing to their tramping carelessly through the streams, was at a standstill. Croquet had been given up in despair.

Near Epping the Russians shot a fox....

The situation which faced Prince Otto was a delicate one. All his early training and education had implanted in him the fixed idea that, if he ever invaded England, he would do it either alone or with the sympathetic co-operation of allies. He had never faced the problem of what he should do if there were rivals in the field. Competition is wholesome, but only within bounds. He could not very well ask the other nations to withdraw. Nor did he feel inclined to withdraw himself.

"It all comes of this dashed Swoop of the Vulture business," he grumbled, as he paced before his tent, ever and anon pausing to sweep the city below him with his glasses. "I should like to find the fellow who started the idea! Making me look a fool! Still, it's just as bad for the others, thank goodness! Well, Poppenheim?"

Captain von Poppenheim approached and saluted.

"Please, sir, the men say, 'May they bombard London?'"

"Bombard London!"

"Yes, sir; it's always done."

Prince Otto pulled thoughtfully at his moustache.

"Bombard London! It seems—and yet—ah, well, they have few pleasures."

He stood awhile in meditation. So did Captain von Poppenheim. He kicked a pebble. So did Captain von Poppenheim—only a smaller pebble. Discipline is very strict in the German army.

"Poppenheim."

"Sir?"

"Any signs of our—er—competitors?"

"Yes, sir; the Russians are coming up on the left flank, sir. They'll be here in a few hours. Raisuli has been arrested at Purley for stealing chickens. The army of Bollygolla is about ten miles out. No news of the field yet, sir."

The Prince brooded. Then he spoke, unbosoming himself more freely than was his wont in conversation with his staff.

"Between you and me, Pop," he cried impulsively, "I'm dashed sorry we ever started this dashed silly invading business. We thought ourselves dashed smart, working in the dark, and giving no sign till the great pounce, and all that sort of dashed nonsense. Seems to me we've simply dashed well landed ourselves in the dashed soup."

Captain von Poppenheim saluted in sympathetic silence. He and the prince had been old chums at college. A life-long friendship existed between them. He would have liked to have expressed adhesion verbally to his superior officer's remarks. The words "I don't think" trembled on his tongue. But the iron discipline of the German Army gagged him. He saluted again and clicked his heels.

The Prince recovered himself with a strong effort.

"You say the Russians will be here shortly?" he said.

"In a few hours, sir."

"And the men really wish to bombard London?"

"It would be a treat to them, sir."

"Well, well, I suppose if we don't do it, somebody else will. And we got here first."

"Yes, sir."

"Then—"

An orderly hurried up and saluted.

"Telegram, sir."

Absently the Prince opened it. Then his eyes lit up.

"Gotterdammerung!" he said. "I never thought of that. 'Smash up London and provide work for unemployed mending it.—GRAYSON,'" he read. "Poppenheim."

"Sir?"

"Let the bombardment commence."

"Yes, sir."

"And let it continue till the Russians arrive. Then it must stop, or there will be complications."

Captain von Poppenheim saluted, and withdrew.

14

CHAPTER 6

THE BOMBARDMENT OF LONDON

Thus was London bombarded. Fortunately it was August, and there was nobody in town.

Otherwise there might have been loss of life.

CHAPTER 7

A CONFERENCE OF THE POWERS

The Russians, led by General Vodkakoff, arrived at Hampstead half an hour after the bombardment had ceased, and the rest of the invaders, including Raisuli, who had got off on an alibi, dropped in at intervals during the week. By the evening of Saturday, the sixth of August, even the Chinese had limped to the metropolis. And the question now was, What was going to happen? England displayed a polite indifference to the problem. We are essentially a nation of sight-seers. To us the excitement of staring at the invaders was enough. Into the complex international problems to which the situation gave rise it did not occur to us to examine. When you consider that a crowd of five hundred Londoners will assemble in the space of two minutes, abandoning entirely all its other business, to watch a cab-horse that has fallen in the street, it is not surprising that the spectacle of nine separate and distinct armies in the metropolis left no room in the British mind for other reflections.

The attraction was beginning to draw people back to London now. They found that the German shells had had one excellent result, they had demolished nearly all the London statues. And what might have conceivably seemed a draw-back, the fact that they had blown great holes in the wood-paving, passed unnoticed amidst the more extensive operations of the London County Council.

Taking it for all in all, the German gunners had simply been beautifying London. The Albert Hall, struck by a merciful shell, had come down with a run, and was now a heap of picturesque ruins; Whitefield's Tabernacle was a charred mass; and the burning of the Royal Academy proved a great comfort to all. At a mass meeting in Trafalgar Square a hearty vote of thanks was passed, with acclamation, to Prince Otto.

But if Londoners rejoiced, the invaders were very far from doing so. The complicated state of foreign politics made it imperative that there should be no friction between the Powers. Yet here a great number of them were in perhaps as embarrassing a position as ever diplomatists were called upon to unravel. When nine dogs are assembled round one bone, it is rarely on the bone alone that teeth-marks are found at the close of the proceedings.

Prince Otto of Saxe-Pfennig set himself resolutely to grapple with the problem. His chance of grappling successfully with it was not improved by the stream of telegrams which arrived daily from his Imperial Master, demanding to know whether he had yet subjugated the country, and if not, why not. He had replied guardedly, stating the difficulties which lay in his way, and had received the following: "At once mailed fist display. On Get or out Get.—WILHELM."

It was then that the distracted prince saw that steps must be taken at once.

Carefully-worded letters were despatched by District Messenger boys to the other generals. Towards nightfall the replies began to come in, and, having read them, the Prince saw that this business could never be settled without a personal interview. Many of the replies were absolutely incoherent.

Raisuli, apologising for delay on the ground that he had been away in the Isle of Dogs cracking a crib, wrote suggesting that the Germans and Moroccans should combine with a view to playing the Confidence Trick on the Swiss general, who seemed a simple sort of chap. "Reminds me of dear old Maclean," wrote Raisuli. "There is money in this. Will you come in? Wire in the morning."

The general of the Monaco forces thought the best way would be to settle the thing by means of a game of chance of the odd-man-out class. He knew a splendid game called Slippery Sam. He could teach them the rules in half a minute.

The reply of Prince Ping Pong Pang of China was probably brilliant and scholarly, but it was expressed in Chinese characters of the Ming period, which Prince Otto did not understand; and even if he had it would have done him no good, for he tried to read it from the top downwards instead of from the bottom up.

The Young Turks, as might have been expected, wrote in their customary flippant, cheeky style. They were full of mischief, as usual. The body of the letter, scrawled in a round, schoolboy hand, dealt principally with the details of the booby-trap which the general had successfully laid for his head of staff. "He was frightfully shirty," concluded the note jubilantly.

From the Bollygolla camp the messenger-boy returned

without a scalp, and with a verbal message to the effect that the King could neither read nor write.

Grand Duke Vodkakoff, from the Russian lines, replied in his smooth, cynical, Russian way:—"You appear anxious, my dear prince, to scratch the other entrants. May I beg you to remember what happens when you scratch a Russian?"

As for the Mad Mullah's reply, it was simply pure delirium. The journey from Somaliland, and his meeting with his friend Mr. Dillon, appeared to have had the worse effects on his sanity. He opened with the statement that he was a tea-pot: and that was the only really coherent remark he made.

Prince Otto placed a hand wearily on his throbbing brow.

"We must have a conference," he said. "It is the only way."

Next day eight invitations to dinner went out from the German camp.

It would be idle to say that the dinner, as a dinner, was a complete success. Half-way through the Swiss general missed his diamond solitaire, and cold glances were cast at Raisuli, who sat on his immediate left. Then the King of Bollygolla's table-manners were frankly inelegant. When he wanted a thing, he grabbed for it. And he seemed to want nearly everything. Nor was the behaviour of the leader of the Young Turks all that could be desired. There had been some talk of only allowing him to come down to dessert; but he had squashed in, as he briefly put it, and it would be paltering with the truth to say that he had not had far more champagne than was good for him. Also, the general of Monaco had brought a pack of cards with him, and was spoiling the harmony by trying to induce Prince Ping Pong Pang to find the lady. And the brainless laugh of the Mad Mullah was very trying.

Altogether Prince Otto was glad when the cloth was removed, and the waiters left the company to smoke and talk business.

Anyone who has had anything to do with the higher diplomacy is aware that diplomatic language stands in a class by itself. It is a language specially designed to deceive the chance listener.

Thus when Prince Otto, turning to Grand Duke Vodkakoff, said quietly, "I hear the crops are coming on nicely down Kent way," the habitual frequenter of diplomatic circles would have understood, as did the Grand Duke, that what he really meant was, "Now about this business. What do you propose to do?"

The company, with the exception of the representative of the Young Turks, who was drinking creme de menthe out of a tumbler,

18

the Mullah and the King of Bollygolla bent forward, deeply interested, to catch the Russian's reply. Much would depend on this.

Vodkakoff carelessly flicked the ash off his cigarette.

"So I hear," he said slowly. "But in Shropshire, they tell me, they are having trouble with the mangel-wurzels."

The prince frowned at this typical piece of shifty Russian diplomacy.

"How is your Highness getting on with your Highness's roller-skating?" he enquired guardedly.

The Russian smiled a subtle smile.

"Poorly," he said, "poorly. The last time I tried the outside edge I thought somebody had thrown the building at me."

Prince Otto flushed. He was a plain, blunt man, and he hated this beating about the bush.

"Why does a chicken cross the road?" he demanded, almost angrily.

The Russian raised his eyebrows, and smiled, but made no reply. The prince, resolved to give him no chance of wriggling away from the point, pressed him hotly.

"Think of a number," he cried. "Double it. Add ten. Take away the number you first thought of. Divide it by three, and what is the result?"

There was an awed silence. Surely the Russian, expert at evasion as he was, could not parry so direct a challenge as this.

He threw away his cigarette and lit a cigar.

"I understand," he said, with a tinkle of defiance in his voice, "that the Suffragettes, as a last resource, propose to capture Mr. Asquith and sing the Suffragette Anthem to him."

A startled gasp ran round the table.

"Because the higher he flies, the fewer?" asked Prince Otto, with sinister calm.

"Because the higher he flies, the fewer," said the Russian smoothly, but with the smoothness of a treacherous sea.

There was another gasp. The situation was becoming alarmingly tense.

"You are plain-spoken, your Highness," said Prince Otto slowly.

At this moment the tension was relieved by the Young Turk falling off his chair with a crash on to the floor. Everyone jumped up startled. Raisuli took advantage of the confusion to pocket a silver ash-tray.

The interruption had a good effect. Frowns relaxed. The wranglers began to see that they had allowed their feelings to run away with them. It was with a conciliatory smile that Prince Otto, filling the Grand Duke's glass, observed:

"Trumper is perhaps the prettier bat, but I confess I admire Fry's robust driving."

The Russian was won over. He extended his hand.

"Two down and three to play, and the red near the top corner pocket," he said with that half-Oriental charm which he knew so well how to exhibit on occasion.

The two shook hands warmly.

And so it was settled, the Russian having, as we have seen, waived his claim to bombard London in his turn, there was no obstacle to a peaceful settlement. It was obvious that the superior forces of the Germans and Russians gave them, if they did but combine, the key to the situation. The decision they arrived at was, as set forth above, as follows. After the fashion of the moment, the Russian and German generals decided to draw the Colour Line. That meant that the troops of China, Somaliland, Bollygolla, as well as Raisuli and the Young Turks, were ruled out. They would be given a week in which to leave the country. Resistance would be useless. The combined forces of the Germans, Russians, Swiss, and Monacoans were overwhelming, especially as the Chinese had not recovered from their wanderings in Wales and were far too footsore still to think of serious fighting.

When they had left, the remaining four Powers would continue the invasion jointly.

Prince Otto of Saxe-Pfennig went to bed that night, comfortably conscious of a good work well done. He saw his way now clear before him.

But he had made one miscalculation. He had not reckoned with Clarence Chugwater.

PART TWO

CHAPTER 1

IN THE BOY SCOUTS' CAMP

Night!

Night in Aldwych!

In the centre of that vast tract of unreclaimed prairie known to Londoners as the Aldwych Site there shone feebly, seeming almost to emphasise the darkness and desolation of the scene, a single light.

It was the camp-fire of the Boy Scouts.

The night was raw and windy. A fine rain had been falling for some hours. The date of September the First. For just a month England had been in the grip of the invaders. The coloured section of the hostile force had either reached its home by now, or was well on its way. The public had seen it go with a certain regret. Not since the visit of the Shah had such an attractive topic of conversation been afforded them. Several comic journalists had built up a reputation and a large price per thousand words on the King of Bollygolla alone. Theatres had benefited by the index of a large, new, unsophisticated public. A piece at the Waldorf Theatre had run for a whole fortnight, and "The Merry Widow" had taken on a new lease of life. Selfridge's, abandoning its policy of caution, had advertised to the extent of a quarter of a column in two weekly papers.

Now the Young Turks were back at school in Constantinople, shuffling their feet and throwing ink pellets at one another; Raisuli, home again in the old mountains, was working up the kidnapping

21

business, which had fallen off sadly in his absence under the charge of an incompetent locum tenens; and the Chinese, the Bollygollans, and the troops of the Mad Mullah were enduring the miseries of sea-sickness out in mid-ocean.

The Swiss army had also gone home, in order to be in time for the winter hotel season. There only remained the Germans, the Russians, and the troops of Monaco.

In the camp of the Boy Scouts a vast activity prevailed.

Few of London's millions realise how tremendous and far-reaching an association the Boy Scouts are. It will be news to the Man in the Street to learn that, with the possible exception of the Black Hand, the Scouts are perhaps the most carefully-organised secret society in the world.

Their ramifications extend through the length and breadth of England. The boys you see parading the streets with hockey-sticks are but a small section, the aristocrats of the Society. Every boy in England, and many a man, is in the pay of the association. Their funds are practically unlimited. By the oath of initiation which he takes on joining, every boy is compelled to pay into the common coffers a percentage of his pocket-money or his salary. When you drop his weekly three and sixpence into the hand of your office-boy on Saturday, possibly you fancy he takes it home to mother. He doesn't. He spend two-and-six on Woodbines. The other shilling goes into the treasury of the Boy Scouts. When you visit your nephew at Eton, and tip him five pounds or whatever it is, does he spend it at the sock-shop? Apparently, yes. In reality, a quarter reaches the common fund.

Take another case, to show the Boy Scouts' power. You are a City merchant, and, arriving at the office one morning in a bad temper, you proceed to cure yourself by taking it out of the office-boy. He says nothing, apparently does nothing. But that evening, as you are going home in the Tube, a burly working-man treads heavily on your gouty foot. In Ladbroke Grove a passing hansom splashes you with mud. Reaching home, you find that the cat has been at the cold chicken and the butler has given notice. You do not connect these things, but they are all alike the results of your unjust behaviour to your office-boy in the morning. Or, meeting a ragged little matchseller, you pat his head and give him six-pence. Next day an anonymous present of champagne arrives at your address.

Terrible in their wrath, the Boy Scouts never forget kindness.

The whistle of a Striped Iguanodon sounded softly in the darkness. The sentry, who was pacing to and fro before the camp-fire, halted, and peered into the night. As he peered, he uttered the plaintive note of a zebra calling to its mate.

22

A voice from the darkness said, "Een gonyama-gonyama."

"Invooboo," replied the sentry argumentatively "Yah bo! Yah bo! Invooboo."

An indistinct figure moved forward.

"Who goes there?"

"A friend."

"Advance, friend, and give the countersign."

"Remember Mafeking, and death to Injuns."

"Pass friend! All's well."

The figure walked on into the firelight. The sentry started; then saluted and stood to attention. On his face was a worshipping look of admiration and awe, such as some young soldier of the Grande Armee might have worn on seeing Napoleon; for the newcomer was Clarence Chugwater.

"Your name?" said Clarence, eyeing the sturdy young warrior.

"Private William Buggins, sir."

"You watch well, Private Buggins. England has need of such as you."

He pinched the young Scout's ear tolerantly. The sentry flushed with pleasure.

"My orders have been carried out?" said Clarence.

"Yes, sir. The patrols are all here."

"Enumerate them."

"The Chinchilla Kittens, the Bongos, the Zebras, the Iguanodons, the Welsh Rabbits, the Snapping Turtles, and a half-patrol of the 33rd London Gazekas, sir."

Clarence nodded.

"'Tis well," he said. "What are they doing?"

"Some of them are acting a Scout's play, sir; some are doing Cone Exercises; one or two are practising deep breathing; and the rest are dancing an Old English Morris Dance."

Clarence nodded.

"They could not be better employed. Inform them that I have arrived and would address them."

The sentry saluted.

Standing in an attitude of deep thought, with his feet apart, his hands clasped behind him, and his chin sunk upon his breast, Clarence made a singularly impressive picture. He had left his Essex home three weeks before, on the expiration of his ten days' holiday, to return to his post of junior sub-reporter on the staff of a leading London evening paper. It was really only at night now that he got any time to himself. During the day his time was his paper's, and he was compelled to spend the weary hours reading off results of races and other sporting items on the tape-machine. It was only at 6 p.m. that he could begin to devote himself to the service of his country.

The Scouts had assembled now, and were standing, keen and alert, ready to do Clarence's bidding.

Clarence returned their salute moodily.

"Scout-master Wagstaff," he said.

The Scout-master, the leader of the troop formed by the various patrols, stepped forward.

"Let the war-dance commence."

Clarence watched the evolutions absently. His heart was ill-attuned to dances. But the thing had to be done, so it was as well to get it over. When the last movement had been completed, he raised his hand.

"Men," he said, in his clear, penetrating alto, "although you have not the same facilities as myself for hearing the latest news, you are all, by this time, doubtless aware that this England of ours lies 'neath the proud foot of a conqueror. It is for us to save her. (Cheers, and a voice "Invooboo!") I would call on you here and now to seize your hockey-sticks and rush upon the invader, were it not, alas! that such an action would merely result in your destruction. At present the invader is too strong. We must wait; and something tells me that we shall not have to wait long. (Applause.) Jealousy is beginning to spring up between the Russians and the Germans. It will be our task to aggravate this feeling. With our perfect organisation this should be easy. Sooner or later this smouldering jealousy is going to burst into flame. Any day now," he proceeded, warming as he spoke, "there may be the dickens of a dust-up between these Johnnies, and then we've got 'em where the hair's short. See what I mean, you chaps? It's like this. Any moment they may start scrapping and chaw each other up, and then we'll simply sail in and knock what's left endways."

A shout of applause went up from the assembled scouts.

"What I am anxious to impress upon you men," concluded Clarence, in more measured tones, "is that our hour approaches. England looks to us, and it is for us to see that she does not look in vain. Sedulously feeding the growing flame of animosity between the component parts of the invading horde, we may contrive to bring about that actual disruption. Till that day, see to it that you prepare yourselves for war. Men, I have finished."

"What the Chief Scout means," said Scout-master Wagstaff, "is no rotting about and all that sort of rot. Jolly well keep yourselves fit, and then, when the time comes, we'll give these Russian and German blighters about the biggest hiding they've ever heard of. Follow the idea? Very well, then. Mind you don't go mucking the show up."

"Een gonyama-gonyama!" shouted the new thoroughly roused troops. "Invooboo! Yah bo! Yah bo! Invooboo!"

The voice of Young England—of Young England alert and at its post!

CHAPTER 2

AN IMPORTANT ENGAGEMENT

Historians, when they come to deal with the opening years of the twentieth century, will probably call this the Music-Hall Age. At the time of the great invasion the music-halls dominated England. Every town and every suburb had its Hall, most of them more than one. The public appetite for sight-seeing had to be satisfied somehow, and the music-hall provided the easiest way of doing it. The Halls formed a common place on which the celebrity and the ordinary man could meet. If an impulsive gentleman slew his grandmother with a coal-hammer, only a small portion of the public could gaze upon his pleasing features at the Old Bailey. To enable the rest to enjoy the intellectual treat, it was necessary to engage him, at enormous expense, to appear at a music-hall. There, if he happened to be acquitted, he would come on the stage, preceded by an asthmatic introducer, and beam affably at the public for ten minutes, speaking at intervals in a totally inaudible voice, and then retire; to be followed by some enterprising lady who had endeavoured, unsuccessfully, to solve the problem of living at the rate of ten thousand a year on an income of nothing, or who had performed some other similarly brainy feat.

It was not till the middle of September that anyone conceived what one would have thought the obvious idea of offering music-hall engagements to the invading generals.

The first man to think of it was Solly Quhayne, the rising young agent. Solly was the son of Abraham Cohen, an eminent agent of the Victorian era. His brothers, Abe Kern, Benjamin Colquhoun, Jack Coyne, and Barney Cowan had gravitated to the City; but Solly had carried on the old business, and was making a big name for himself. It was Solly who had met Blinky Bill Mullins, the prominent sand-bagger, as he emerged from his twenty years' retirement at Dartmoor, and booked him solid for a thirty-six months' lecturing tour on the McGinnis circuit. It was to him, too, that Joe Brown, who could eat eight pounds of raw meat in seven and a quarter minutes, owed his first chance of displaying his gifts to the wider public of the vaudeville stage.

The idea of securing the services of the invading generals came to him in a flash.

"S'elp me!" he cried. "I believe they'd go big; put 'em on where you like."

Solly was a man of action. Within a minute he was talking to the managing director of the Mammoth Syndicate Halls on the telephone. In five minutes the managing director had agreed to pay Prince Otto of Saxe-Pfennig five hundred pounds a week, if he could be prevailed upon to appear. In ten minutes the Grand Duke Vodkakoff had been engaged, subject to his approval, at a weekly four hundred and fifty by the Stone-Rafferty circuit. And in a quarter of an hour Solly Quhayne, having pushed his way through a mixed crowd of Tricky Serios and Versatile Comedians and Patterers who had been waiting to see him for the last hour and a half, was bowling off in a taximeter-cab to the Russian lines at Hampstead.

General Vodkakoff received his visitor civilly, but at first without enthusiasm. There were, it seemed, objections to his becoming an artiste. Would he have to wear a properly bald head and sing songs about wanting people to see his girl? He didn't think he could. He had only sung once in his life, and that was twenty years ago at a bump-supper at Moscow University. And even then, he confided to Mr. Quhayne, it had taken a decanter and a-half of neat vodka to bring him up to the scratch.

The agent ridiculed the idea.

"Why, your Grand Grace," he cried, "there won't be anything of that sort. You ain't going to be starred as a comic. You're a Refined Lecturer and Society Monologue Artist. 'How I Invaded England,' with lights down and the cinematograph going. We can easily fake the pictures."

The Grand Duke made another objection.

"I understand," he said, "it is etiquette for music-hall artists in their spare time to eat—er—fried fish with their fingers. Must I do that? I doubt if I could manage it."

Mr Quhayne once more became the human semaphore.

"S'elp me! Of course you needn't! All the leading pros, eat it with a spoon. Bless you, you can be the refined gentleman on the Halls same as anywhere else. Come now, your Grand Grace, is it a deal? Four hundred and fifty chinking o'Goblins a week for one hall a night, and press-agented at eight hundred and seventy-five. S'elp me! Lauder doesn't get it, not in England."

The Grand Duke reflected. The invasion has proved more expensive than he had foreseen. The English are proverbially a nation of shopkeepers, and they had put up their prices in all the shops for his special benefit. And he was expected to do such a lot of tipping. Four hundred and fifty a week would come in uncommonly useful.

"Where do I sign?" he asked, extending his hand for the agreement.

Five minutes later Mr. Quhayne was urging his taxidriver to exceed the speed-limit in the direction of Tottenham.

CHAPTER 3

A BIRD'S-EYE VIEW OF THE SITUATION

Clarence read the news of the two engagements on the tape at the office of his paper, but the first intimation the general public had of it was through the medium of headlines:—

MUSIC-HALL SENSATION
INVADING GENERALS' GIGANTIC SALARIES
RUMOURED RESENTMENT OF V.A.F.
WHAT WILL WATER-RATS DO?
INTERVIEW WITH MR. HARRY LAUDER

Clarence chuckled grimly as the tape clicked out the news. The end had begun. To sow jealousy between the rival generals would have been easy. To sow it between two rival music-hall artistes would be among the world's softest jobs.

Among the general public, of course, the announcement created a profound sensation. Nothing else was talked about in train and omnibus. The papers had leaders on the subject. At first the popular impression was that the generals were going to do a comedy duo act of the Who-Was-It-I-Seen-You-Coming-Down-the-Street-With? type, and there was disappointment when it was found that the engagements were for different halls. Rumours sprang up. It was said that the Grand Duke had for years been an enthusiastic amateur sword-swallower, and had, indeed, come to England mainly for the purpose of getting bookings; that the Prince had a secure reputation in Potsdam as a singer of songs in the George Robey style; that both were expert trick-cyclists.

Then the truth came out. Neither had any specialities; they would simply appear and deliver lectures.

The feeling in the music-hall world was strong. The Variety Artists' Federation debated the advisability of another strike. The Water Rats, meeting in mystic secrecy in a Maiden Lane public-house, passed fifteen resolutions in an hour and a quarter. Sir Harry Lauder, interviewed by the Era, gave it as his opinion that both the Grand Duke and the Prince were gowks, who would do well to haud their blether. He himself proposed to go straight to America, where genuine artists were cheered in the streets and entertained at haggis dinners, and not forced to compete with amateur sumphs and gonuphs from other countries.

Clarence, brooding over the situation like a Providence, was glad to see that already the new move had weakened the invaders' power. The day after the announcement in the press of the approaching debut of the other generals, the leader of the army of Monaco had hurried to the agents to secure an engagement for himself. He held out the special inducement of card-tricks, at which he was highly skilled. The agents had received him coldly. Brown and Day had asked him to call again. Foster had sent out a message regretting that he was too busy to see him. At de Freece's he had been kept waiting in the ante-room for two hours in the midst of a bevy of Sparkling Comediennes of pronounced peroxidity and blue-chinned men in dusty bowler-hats, who told each other how they had gone with a bang at Oakham and John o'Groats, and had then gone away in despair.

On the following day, deeply offended, he had withdrawn his troops from the country.

The strength of the invaders was melting away little by little.

"How long?" murmured Clarence Chugwater, as he worked at the tape-machine. "How long?"

CHAPTER 4

CLARENCE HEARS IMPORTANT NEWS

It was Clarence's custom to leave the office of his newspaper at one o'clock each day, and lunch at a neighbouring Aerated Bread shop. He did this on the day following the first appearance of the two generals at their respective halls. He had brought an early edition of the paper with him, and in the intervals of dealing with his glass of milk and scone and butter, he read the report of the performances.

Both, it seemed, had met with flattering receptions, though they had appeared nervous. The Russian general especially, whose style, said the critic, was somewhat reminiscent of Mr. T. E. Dunville, had made himself a great favourite with the gallery. The report concluded by calling attention once more to the fact that the salaries paid to the two—eight hundred and seventy-five pounds a week each—established a record in music-hall history on this side of the Atlantic.

Clarence had just finished this when there came to his ear the faint note of a tarantula singing to its young.

He looked up. Opposite him, at the next table, was seated a youth of fifteen, of a slightly grubby aspect. He was eyeing Clarence closely.

Clarence took off his spectacles, polished them, and replaced them on his nose. As he did so, the thin gruffle of the tarantula sounded once more. Without changing his expression, Clarence cautiously uttered the deep snarl of a sand-eel surprised while bathing.

It was sufficient. The other rose to his feet, holding his right hand on a line with his shoulder, palm to the front, thumb resting on the nail of the little finger, and the other three fingers upright.

Clarence seized his hat by the brim at the back, and moved it swiftly twice up and down.

The other, hesitating no longer, came over to his table.

"Pip-pip!" he said, in an undertone.

"Toodleoo and God save the King!" whispered Clarence.

The mystic ceremony which always takes place when two Boy Scouts meet in public was complete.

"Private Biggs of the Eighteenth Tarantulas, sir," said the boy respectfully, for he had recognised Clarence.

Clarence inclined his head.

"You may sit, Private Biggs," he said graciously. "You have news to impart?"

"News, sir, that may be of vital importance."

"Say on."

Private Biggs, who had brought his sparkling limado and a bath-bun with him from the other table, took a sip of the former, and embarked upon his narrative.

"I am employed, sir," he said, "as a sort of junior clerk and office-boy by Mr. Solly Quhayne, the music-hall agent."

Clarence tapped his brow thoughtfully; then his face cleared.

"I remember. It was he who secured the engagements of the generals."

"The same, sir."

"Proceed."

The other resumed his story.

"It is my duty to sit in a sort of rabbit-hutch in the outer office, take the callers' names, and especially to see that they don't get through to Mr. Quhayne till he wishes to receive them. That is the most exacting part of my day's work. You wouldn't believe how full of the purest swank some of these pros. are. Tell you they've got an appointment as soon as look at you. Artful beggars!"

Clarence nodded sympathetically.

"This morning an Acrobat and Society Contortionist made such a fuss that in the end I had to take his card in to the private office. Mr. Quhayne was there talking to a gentleman whom I recognised as his brother, Mr. Colquhoun. They were engrossed in their conversation, and did not notice me for a moment. With no wish to play the eavesdropper, I could not help but overhear. They were talking about the generals. 'Yes, I know they're press-agented at eight seventy-five, dear boy,' I heard Mr. Quhayne say, 'but between you and me and the door-knob that isn't what they're getting. The German feller's drawing five hundred of the best, but I could only get four-fifty for the Russian. Can't say why. I should have thought, if anything, he'd be the bigger draw. Bit of a comic in his way!' And then he saw me. There was some slight unpleasantness. In fact, I've got the sack. After it was over I came away to try and find you. It seemed to me that the information might be of importance."

Clarence's eyes gleamed.

"You have done splendidly, Private—no, Corporal Biggs. Do not regret your lost position. The society shall find you work. This news you have brought is of the utmost—the most vital importance. Dash it!" he cried, unbending in his enthusiasm, "we've got 'em on the hop. If they aren't biting pieces out of each other in the next day or two, I'm jolly well mistaken."

He rose; then sat down again.

"Corporal—no, dash it, Sergeant Biggs—you must have something with me. This is an occasion. The news you have brought me may mean the salvation of England. What would you like?"

The other saluted joyfully.

"I think I'll have another sparkling limado, thanks, awfully," he said.

The beverage arrived. They raised their glasses.

"To England," said Clarence simply.

"To England," echoed his subordinate.

Clarence left the shop with swift strides, and hurried, deep in thought, to the offices of the Encore in Wellington Street.

"Yus?" said the office-boy interrogatively.

Clarence gave the Scout's Siquand, the pass-word. The boy's demeanour changed instantly. He saluted with the utmost respect.

"I wish to see the Editor," said Clarence.

A short speech, but one that meant salvation for the motherland.

CHAPTER 5

SEEDS OF DISCORD

The days following Clarence's visit to the offices of the Encore were marked by a growing feeling of unrest, alike among invaded and invaders. The first novelty and excitement of the foreign occupation of the country was beginning to wear off, and in its place the sturdy independence so typical of the British character was reasserting itself. Deep down in his heart the genuine Englishman has a rugged distaste for seeing his country invaded by a foreign army. People were asking themselves by what right these aliens had overrun British soil. An ever-growing feeling of annoyance had begun to lay hold of the nation.

It is probable that the departure of Sir Harry Lauder first brought home to England what this invasion might mean. The great comedian, in his manifesto in the Times, had not minced his words. Plainly and crisply he had stated that he was leaving the country because the music-hall stage was given over to alien gowks. He was sorry for England. He liked England. But now, all he could say was, "God bless you." England shuddered, remembering that last time he had said, "God bless you till I come back."

Ominous mutterings began to make themselves heard.

Other causes contributed to swell the discontent. A regiment of Russians, out route-marching, had walked across the bowling-screen at Kennington Oval during the Surrey v. Lancashire match, causing Hayward to be bowled for a duck's-egg. A band of German sappers had dug a trench right across the turf at Queen's Club.

The mutterings increased.

Nor were the invaders satisfied and happy. The late English summer had set in with all its usual severity, and the Cossacks, reared in the kindlier climate of Siberia, were feeling it terribly. Colds were the rule rather than the exception in the Russian lines. The coughing of the Germans at Tottenham could be heard in Oxford Street.

The attitude of the British public, too, was getting on their nerves. They had been prepared for fierce resistance. They had pictured the invasion as a series of brisk battles—painful perhaps, but exciting. They had anticipated that when they had conquered the country they might meet with the Glare of Hatred as they patrolled the streets. The Supercilious Stare unnerved them. There is nothing so terrible to the highly-strung foreigner as the cold, contemptuous, patronising gaze of the Englishman. It gave the invaders a perpetual feeling of doing the wrong thing. They felt like men who had been found travelling in a first-class carriage with a third-class ticket. They became conscious of the size of their hands and feet. As they marched through the Metropolis they felt their ears growing hot and red. Beneath the chilly stare of the populace they experienced all the sensations of a man who has come to a strange dinner-party in a tweed suit when everybody else has dressed. They felt warm and prickly.

It was dull for them, too. London is never at its best in early September, even for the habitue. There was nothing to do. Most of the theatres were shut. The streets were damp and dirty. It was all very well for the generals, appearing every night in the glare and glitter of the footlights; but for the rank and file the occupation of London spelt pure boredom.

London was, in fact, a human powder-magazine. And it was Clarence Chugwater who with a firm hand applied the match that was to set it in a blaze.

CHAPTER 6

THE BOMB-SHELL

Clarence had called at the offices of the Encore on a Friday. The paper's publishing day is Thursday. The Encore is the Times of the music-hall world. It casts its curses here, bestows its benedictions (sparely) there. The Encore criticising the latest action of the Variety Artists' Federation is the nearest modern approach to Jove hurling the thunderbolt. Its motto is, "Cry havoc, and let loose the performing dogs of war."

It so happened that on the Thursday following his momentous visit to Wellington Street, there was need of someone on the staff of Clarence's evening paper to go and obtain an interview from the Russian general. Mr. Hubert Wales had just published a novel so fruity in theme and treatment that it had been publicly denounced from the pulpit by no less a person than the Rev. Canon Edgar Sheppard, D.D., Sub-Dean of His Majesty's Chapels Royal, Deputy Clerk of the Closet and Sub-Almoner to the King. A morning paper had started the question, "Should there be a Censor of Fiction?" and, in accordance with custom, editors were collecting the views of celebrities, preferably of those whose opinion on the subject was absolutely valueless.

All the other reporters being away on their duties, the editor was at a loss.

"Isn't there anybody else?" he demanded.

The chief sub-editor pondered.

"There is young blooming Chugwater," he said.

(It was thus that England's deliverer was habitually spoken of in the office.)

"Then send him," said the editor.

Grand Duke Vodkakoff's turn at the Magnum Palace of Varieties started every evening at ten sharp. He topped the bill. Clarence, having been detained by a review of the Scouts, did not reach the hall till five minutes to the hour. He got to the dressing-room as the general was going on to the stage.

The Grand Duke dressed in the large room with the other male turns. There were no private dressing-rooms at the Magnum. Clarence sat down on a basket-trunk belonging to the Premier Troupe of Bounding Zouaves of the Desert, and waited. The four athletic young gentlemen who composed the troupe were dressing after their turn. They took no notice of Clarence.

Presently one Zouave spoke.

"Bit off to-night, Bill. Cold house."

"Not 'arf," replied his colleague. "Gave me the shivers."

"Wonder how his nibs'll go."

Evidently he referred to the Grand Duke.

"Oh, 'e's all right. They eat his sort of swank. Seems to me the profession's going to the dogs, what with these bloomin' amytoors an' all. Got the 'airbrush, 'Arry?"

Harry, a tall, silent Zouave, handed over the hairbrush.

Bill continued.

"I'd like to see him go on of a Monday night at the old Mogul. They'd soon show him. It gives me the fair 'ump, it does, these toffs coming in and taking the bread out of our mouths. Why can't he give us chaps a chance? Fair makes me rasp, him and his bloomin' eight hundred and seventy-five o' goblins a week."

"Not so much of your eight hundred and seventy-five, young feller me lad," said the Zouave who had spoken first. "Ain't you seen the rag this week?"

"Naow. What's in it? How does our advert, look?"

"Ow, that's all right, never mind that. You look at 'What the Encore Would Like to Know.' That's what'll touch his nibs up."

He produced a copy of the paper from the pocket of his great-coat which hung from the door, and passed it to his bounding brother.

"Read it out, old sort," he said.

The other took it to the light and began to read slowly and cautiously, as one who is no expert at the art.

"'What the Encore would like to know:—Whether Prince Otto of Saxe-Pfennig didn't go particularly big at the Lobelia last week? And Whether his success hasn't compelled Agent Quhayne to purchase a larger-sized hat? And Whether it isn't a fact that, though they are press-agented at the same figure, Prince Otto is getting fifty a week more than Grand Duke Vodkakoff? And If it is not so, why a little bird has assured us that the Prince is being paid five hundred a week and the Grand Duke only four hundred and fifty? And, In any case, whether the Prince isn't worth fifty a week more than his Russian friend?' Lumme!"

An awed silence fell upon the group. To Clarence, who had dictated the matter (though the style was the editor's), the paragraph did not come as a surprise. His only feeling was one of relief that the editor had served up his material so well. He felt that he had been justified in leaving the more delicate literary work to that master-hand.

"That'll be one in the eye," said the Zouave Harry. "'Ere, I'll stick it up opposite of him when he comes back to dress. Got a pin and a pencil, some of you?"

He marked the quarter column heavily, and pinned it up beside the looking-glass. Then he turned to his companions.

"'Ow about not waiting, chaps?" he suggested. "I shouldn't 'arf wonder, from the look of him, if he wasn't the 'aughty kind of a feller who'd cleave you to the bazooka for tuppence with his bloomin' falchion. I'm goin' to 'urry through with my dressing and wait till to-morrow night to see how he looks. No risks for Willie!"

The suggestion seemed thoughtful and good. The Bounding Zouaves, with one accord, bounded into their clothes and disappeared through the door just as a long-drawn chord from the invisible orchestra announced the conclusion of the Grand Duke's turn.

General Vodkakoff strutted into the room, listening complacently to the applause which was still going on. He had gone well. He felt pleased with himself.

It was not for a moment that he noticed Clarence.

"Ah," he said, "the interviewer, eh? You wish to—"

Clarence began to explain his mission. While he was doing so the Grand Duke strolled to the basin and began to remove his make-up. He favoured, when on the stage, a touch of the Raven Gipsy No. 3 grease-paint. It added a picturesque swarthiness to his appearance, and made him look more like what he felt to be the popular ideal of a Russian general.

The looking-glass hung just over the basin.

Clarence, watching him in the glass, saw him start as he read the first paragraph. A dark flush, almost rivalling the Raven Gipsy No. 3, spread over his face. He trembled with rage.

"Who put that paper there?" he roared, turning.

"With reference, then, to Mr. Hubert Wales's novel," said Clarence.

The Grand Duke cursed Mr. Hubert Wales, his novel, and Clarence in one sentence.

"You may possibly," continued Clarence, sticking to his point like a good interviewer, "have read the trenchant, but some say justifiable remarks of the Rev. Canon Edgar Sheppard, D.D., Sub-Dean of His Majesty's Chapels Royal, Deputy Clerk of the Closet, and Sub-Almoner to the King."

The Grand Duke swiftly added that eminent cleric to the list.

"Did you put that paper on this looking-glass?" he shouted.

"I did not put that paper on that looking-glass," replied Clarence precisely.

"Ah," said the Grand Duke, "if you had, I'd have come and wrung your neck like a chicken, and scattered you to the four corners of this dressing-room."

"I'm glad I didn't," said Clarence.

"Have you read this paper on the looking-glass?"

"I have not read that paper on the looking-glass," replied Clarence, whose chief fault as a conversationalist was that he was perhaps a shade too Ollendorfian. "But I know its contents."

"It's a lie!" roared the Grand Duke. "An infamous lie! I've a good mind to have him up for libel. I know very well he got them to put those paragraphs in, if he didn't write them himself."

"Professional jealousy," said Clarence, with a sigh, "is a very sad thing."

"I'll professional jealousy him!"

"I hear," said Clarence casually, "that he has been going very well at the Lobelia. A friend of mine who was there last night told me he took eleven calls."

For a moment the Russian General's face swelled apoplectically. Then he recovered himself with a tremendous effort.

"Wait!" he said, with awful calm. "Wait till to-morrow night! I'll show him! Went very well, did he? Ha! Took eleven calls, did he? Oh, ha, ha! And he'll take them to-morrow night, too! Only"—and here his voice took on a note of fiendish purpose so terrible that, hardened scout as he was, Clarence felt his flesh creep—"only this time they'll be catcalls!"

And, with a shout of almost maniac laughter, the jealous artiste flung himself into a chair, and began to pull off his boots.

Clarence silently withdrew. The hour was very near.

CHAPTER 7

THE BIRD

The Grand Duke Vodkakoff was not the man to let the grass grow under his feet. He was no lobster, no flat-fish. He did it now—swift, secret, deadly—a typical Muscovite. By midnight his staff had their orders.

Those orders were for the stalls at the Lobelia.

Price of entrance to the gallery and pit was served out at daybreak to the Eighth and Fifteenth Cossacks of the Don, those fierce, semi-civilised fighting-machines who know no fear.

Grand Duke Vodkakoff's preparations were ready.

Few more fortunate events have occurred in the history of English literature than the quite accidental visit of Mr. Bart Kennedy to the Lobelia on that historic night. He happened to turn in there casually after dinner, and was thus enabled to see the whole thing from start to finish. At a quarter to eleven a wild-eyed man charged in at the main entrance of Carmelite House, and, too impatient to use the lift, dashed up the stairs, shouting for pens, ink and paper.

Next morning the Daily Mail was one riot of headlines. The whole of page five was given up to the topic. The headlines were not elusive. They flung the facts at the reader:—

> *SCENE AT THE LOBELIA*
> *PRINCE OTTO OF SAXE-PFENNIG*
> *GIVEN THE BIRD BY*
> *RUSSIAN SOLDIERS*
> *WHAT WILL BE THE OUTCOME?*

There were about seventeen more, and then came Mr. Bart Kennedy's special report.

He wrote as follows:—

"A night to remember. A marvellous night. A night such as few

40

will see again. A night of fear and wonder. The night of September the eleventh. Last night.

"Nine-thirty. I had dined. I had eaten my dinner. My dinner! So inextricably are the prose and romance of life blended. My dinner! I had eaten my dinner on this night. This wonderful night. This night of September the eleventh. Last night!

"I had dined at the club. A chop. A boiled potato. Mushrooms on toast. A touch of Stilton. Half-a-bottle of Beaune. I lay back in my chair. I debated within myself. A Hall? A theatre? A book in the library? That night, the night of September the eleventh, I as near as a toucher spent in the library of my club with a book. That night! The night of September the eleventh. Last night!

"Fate took me to the Lobelia. Fate! We are its toys. Its footballs. We are the footballs of Fate. Fate might have sent me to the Gaiety. Fate took me to the Lobelia. This Fate which rules us.

"I sent in my card to the manager. He let me through. Ever courteous. He let me through on my face. This manager. This genial and courteous manager.

"I was in the Lobelia. A dead-head. I was in the Lobelia as a dead-head!"

Here, in the original draft of the article, there are reflections, at some length, on the interior decorations of the Hall, and an excursus on music-hall performances in general. It is not till he comes to examine the audience that Mr. Kennedy returns to the main issue.

"And what manner of audience was it that had gathered together to view the entertainment provided by the genial and courteous manager of the Lobelia? The audience. Beyond whom there is no appeal. The Caesars of the music-hall. The audience."

At this point the author has a few extremely interesting and thoughtful remarks on the subject of audiences. These may be omitted. "In the stalls I noted a solid body of Russian officers. These soldiers from the Steppes. These bearded men. These Russians. They sat silent and watchful. They applauded little. The programme left them cold. The Trick Cyclist. The Dashing Soubrette and Idol of Belgravia. The Argumentative College Chums. The Swell Comedian. The Man with the Performing Canaries. None of these could rouse them. They were waiting. Waiting. Waiting tensely. Every muscle taut. Husbanding their strength. Waiting. For what?

"A man at my side told a friend that a fellow had told him that he had been told by a commissionaire that the pit and gallery were full of Russians. Russians. Russians everywhere. Why? Were they genuine patrons of the Halls? Or were they there from some ulterior motive? There was an air of suspense. We were all waiting. Waiting. For what?

"The atmosphere is summed up in a word. One word. Sinister. The atmosphere was sinister.

"AA! A stir in the crowded house. The ruffling of the face of the sea before a storm. The Sisters Sigsbee, Coon Delineators and Unrivalled Burlesque Artists, have finished their dance, smiled, blown kisses, skipped off, skipped on again, smiled, blown more kisses, and disappeared. A long chord from the orchestra. A chord that is almost a wail. A wail of regret for that which is past. Two liveried menials appear. They carry sheets of cardboard. These menials carry sheets of cardboard. But not blank sheets. On each sheet is a number.

"The number 15.

"Who is number 15?

"Prince Otto of Saxe-Pfennig. Prince Otto, General of the German Army. Prince Otto is Number 15.

"A burst of applause from the house. But not from the Russians. They are silent. They are waiting. For what?

"The orchestra plays a lively air. The massive curtains part. A tall, handsome military figure strides on to the stage. He bows. This tall, handsome, military man bows. He is Prince Otto of Saxe-Pfennig, General of the Army of Germany. One of our conquerors.

"He begins to speak. 'Ladies and gentlemen.' This man, this general, says, 'Ladies and gentlemen.'

"But no more. No more. No more. Nothing more. No more. He says, 'Ladies and Gentlemen,' but no more.

"And why does he say no more? Has he finished his turn? Is that all he does? Are his eight hundred and seventy-five pounds a week paid him for saying, 'Ladies and Gentlemen'?

"No!

"He would say more. He has more to say. This is only the beginning. This tall, handsome man has all his music still within him.

"Why, then, does he say no more? Why does he say 'Ladies and Gentlemen,' but no more? No more. Only that. No more. Nothing more. No more.

"Because from the stalls a solid, vast, crushing 'Boo!' is hurled at him. From the Russians in the stalls comes this vast, crushing 'Boo!' It is for this that they have been waiting. It is for this that they have been waiting so tensely. For this. They have been waiting for this colossal 'Boo!'"

"The General retreats a step. He is amazed. Startled. Perhaps frightened. He waves his hands.

"From gallery and pit comes a hideous whistling and howling. The noise of wild beasts. The noise of exploding boilers. The noise of a music-hall audience giving a performer the bird.

"Everyone is standing on his feet. Some on mine. Everyone is shouting. This vast audience is shouting.

"Words begin to emerge from the babel.

"'Get offski! Rotten turnovitch!' These bearded Russians, these stern critics, shout, 'Rotten turnovitch!'

"Fire shoots from the eyes of the German. This strong man's eyes.

"'Get offski! Swankietoff! Rotten turnovitch!'

"The fury of this audience is terrible. This audience. This last court of appeal. This audience in its fury is terrible.

"What will happen? The German stands his ground. This man of blood and iron stands his ground. He means to go on. This strong man. He means to go on if it snows.

"The audience is pulling up the benches. A tomato shatters itself on the Prince's right eye. An over-ripe tomato.

"'Get offski!' Three eggs and a cat sail through the air. Falling short, they drop on to the orchestra. These eggs! This cat! They fall on the conductor and the second trombone. They fall like the gentle dew from Heaven upon the place beneath. That cat! Those eggs!

"AA! At last the stage-manager—keen, alert, resourceful—saves the situation. This man. This stage-manager. This man with the big brain. Slowly, inevitably, the fireproof curtain falls. It is half-way down. It is down. Before it, the audience. The audience. Behind it, the Prince. The Prince. That general. That man of iron. That performer who has just got the bird.

"The Russian National Anthem rings through the hall. Thunderous! Triumphant! The Russian National Anthem. A paean of joy.

"The menials reappear. Those calm, passionless menials. They remove the number fifteen. They insert the number sixteen. They are like Destiny—Pitiless, Unmoved, Purposeful, Silent. Those menials.

"A crash from the orchestra. Turn number sixteen has begun...."

CHAPTER 8

THE MEETING AT THE SCOTCH STORES

Prince Otto of Saxe-Pfennig stood in the wings, shaking in every limb. German oaths of indescribable vigour poured from his lips. In a group some feet away stood six muscular, short-sleeved stage-hands. It was they who had flung themselves on the general at the fall of the iron curtain and prevented him dashing round to attack the stalls with his sabre. At a sign from the stage-manager they were ready to do it again.

The stage-manager was endeavouring to administer balm.

"Bless you, your Highness," he was saying, "it's nothing. It's what happens to everyone some time. Ask any of the top-notch pros. Ask 'em whether they never got the bird when they were starting. Why, even now some of the biggest stars can't go to some towns because they always cop it there. Bless you, it——"

A stage-hand came up with a piece of paper in his hand.

"Young feller in spectacles and a rum sort o' suit give me this for your 'Ighness."

The Prince snatched it from his hand.

The note was written in a round, boyish hand. It was signed, "A Friend." It ran:—"The men who booed you to-night were sent for that purpose by General Vodkakoff, who is jealous of you because of the paragraphs in the Encore this week."

Prince Otto became suddenly calm.

"Excuse me, your Highness," said the stage-manager anxiously, as he moved, "you can't go round to the front. Stand by, Bill."

"Right, sir!" said the stage-hands.

Prince Otto smiled pleasantly.

"There is no danger. I do not intend to go to the front. I am going to look in at the Scotch Stores for a moment."

"Oh, in that case, your Highness, good-night, your Highness! Better luck to-morrow, your Highness!"

It had been the custom of the two generals, since they had

44

joined the music-hall profession, to go, after their turn, to the Scotch Stores, where they stood talking and blocking the gangway, as etiquette demands that a successful artiste shall.

The Prince had little doubt but that he would find Vodkakoff there to-night.

He was right. The Russian general was there, chatting affably across the counter about the weather.

He nodded at the Prince with a well-assumed carelessness.

"Go well to-night?" he inquired casually.

Prince Otto clenched his fists; but he had had a rigorously diplomatic up-bringing, and knew how to keep a hold on himself. When he spoke it was in the familiar language of diplomacy.

"The rain has stopped," he said, "but the pavements are still wet underfoot. Has your grace taken the precaution to come out in a good stout pair of boots?"

The shaft plainly went home, but the Grand Duke's manner, as he replied, was unruffled.

"Rain," he said, sipping his vermouth, "is always wet; but sometimes it is cold as well."

"But it never falls upwards," said the Prince, pointedly.

"Rarely, I understand. Your powers of observation are keen, my dear Prince."

There was a silence; then the Prince, momentarily baffled, returned to the attack.

"The quickest way to get from Charing Cross to Hammersmith Broadway," he said, "is to go by Underground."

"Men have died in Hammersmith Broadway," replied the Grand Duke suavely.

The Prince gritted his teeth. He was no match for his slippery adversary in a diplomatic dialogue, and he knew it.

"The sun rises in the East," he cried, half-choking, "but it sets—it sets!"

"So does a hen," was the cynical reply.

The last remnants of the Prince's self-control were slipping away. This elusive, diplomatic conversation is a terrible strain if one is not in the mood for it. Its proper setting is the gay, glittering ball-room at some frivolous court. To a man who has just got the bird at a music-hall, and who is trying to induce another man to confess that the thing was his doing, it is little short of maddening.

"Hen!" he echoed, clenching and unclenching his fists. "Have you studied the habits of hens?"

The truth seemed very near to him now, but the master-

45

diplomat before him was used to extracting himself from awkward corners.

"Pullets with a southern exposure," he drawled, "have yellow legs and ripen quickest."

The Prince was nonplussed. He had no answer.

The girl behind the bar spoke.

"You do talk silly, you two!" she said.

It was enough. Trivial as the remark was, it was the last straw. The Prince brought his fist down with a crash on the counter.

"Yes," he shouted, "you are right. We do talk silly; but we shall do so no longer. I am tired of this verbal fencing. A plain answer to a plain question. Did you or did you not send your troops to give me the bird to-night?"

"My dear Prince!"

The Grand Duke raised his eyebrows.

"Did you or did you not?"

"The wise man," said the Russian, still determined on evasion, "never takes sides, unless they are sides of bacon."

The Prince smashed a glass.

"You did!" he roared. "I know you did! Listen to me! I'll give you one chance. I'll give you and your precious soldiers twenty-four hours from midnight to-night to leave this country. If you are still here then——"

He paused dramatically.

The Grand Duke slowly drained his vermouth.

"Have you seen my professional advertisement in the Era, my dear Prince?" he asked.

"I have. What of it?"

"You noticed nothing about it?"

"I did not."

"Ah. If you had looked more closely, you would have seen the words, 'Permanent address, Hampstead.'"

"You mean——"

"I mean that I see no occasion to alter that advertisement in any way."

There was another tense silence. The two men looked hard at each other.

"That is your final decision?" said the German.

The Russian bowed.

"So be it," said the Prince, turning to the door. "I have the honour to wish you a very good night."

"The same to you," said the Grand Duke. "Mind the step."

CHAPTER 9

THE GREAT BATTLE

The news that an open rupture had occurred between the Generals of the two invading armies was not slow in circulating. The early editions of the evening papers were full of it. A symposium of the opinions of Dr. Emil Reich, Dr. Saleeby, Sandow, Mr. Chiozza Money, and Lady Grove was hastily collected. Young men with knobbly and bulging foreheads were turned on by their editors to write character-sketches of the two generals. All was stir and activity.

Meanwhile, those who look after London's public amusements were busy with telephone and telegraph. The quarrel had taken place on Friday night. It was probable that, unless steps were taken, the battle would begin early on Saturday. Which, it did not require a man of unusual intelligence to see, would mean a heavy financial loss to those who supplied London with its Saturday afternoon amusements. The matinees would suffer. The battle might not affect the stalls and dress-circle, perhaps, but there could be no possible doubt that the pit and gallery receipts would fall off terribly. To the public which supports the pit and gallery of a theatre there is an irresistible attraction about a fight on anything like a large scale. When one considers that a quite ordinary street-fight will attract hundreds of spectators, it will be plainly seen that no theatrical entertainment could hope to compete against so strong a counter-attraction as a battle between the German and Russian armies.

The various football-grounds would be heavily hit, too. And there was to be a monster roller-skating carnival at Olympia. That also would be spoiled.

A deputation of amusement-caterers hurried to the two camps within an hour of the appearance of the first evening paper. They put their case plainly and well. The Generals were obviously impressed. Messages passed and repassed between the two armies, and in the end it was decided to put off the outbreak of hostilities till Monday morning.

Satisfactory as this undoubtedly was for the theatre-managers and directors of football clubs, it was in some ways a pity. From the standpoint of the historian it spoiled the whole affair. But for the postponement, readers of this history might—nay, would—have been able to absorb a vivid and masterly account of the great struggle, with a careful description of the tactics by which victory was achieved. They would have been told the disposition of the various regiments, the stratagems, the dashing advances, the skilful retreats, and the Lessons of the War.

As it is, owing to the mistaken good-nature of the rival generals, the date of the fixture was changed, and practically all that a historian can do is to record the result.

A slight mist had risen as early as four o'clock on Saturday. By night-fall the atmosphere was a little dense, but the lamp-posts were still clearly visible at a distance of some feet, and nobody, accustomed to living in London, would have noticed anything much out of the common. It was not till Sunday morning that the fog proper really began.

London awoke on Sunday to find the world blanketed in the densest, yellowest London particular that had been experienced for years. It was the sort of day when the City clerk has the exhilarating certainty that at last he has an excuse for lateness which cannot possibly be received with harsh disbelief. People spent the day indoors and hoped it would clear up by tomorrow.

"They can't possibly fight if it's like this," they told each other.

But on the Monday morning the fog was, if possible, denser. It wrapped London about as with a garment. People shook their heads.

"They'll have to put it off," they were saying, when of a sudden—Boom! And, again, Boom!

It was the sound of heavy guns.

The battle had begun!

One does not wish to grumble or make a fuss, but still it does seem a little hard that a battle of such importance, a battle so outstanding in the history of the world, should have been fought under such conditions. London at that moment was richer than ever before in descriptive reporters. It was the age of descriptive reporters, of vivid pen-pictures. In every newspaper office there were men who could have hauled up their slacks about that battle in a way that would have made a Y.M.C.A. lecturer want to get at somebody with a bayonet; men who could have handed out the adjectives and exclamation-marks till you almost heard the roar of the guns. And there they were—idle, supine—like careened

48

battleships. They were helpless. Bart Kennedy did start an article which began, "Fog. Black fog. And the roar of guns. Two nations fighting in the fog," but it never came to anything. It was promising for a while, but it died of inanition in the middle of the second stick.

It was hard.

The lot of the actual war-correspondents was still worse. It was useless for them to explain that the fog was too thick to give them a chance. "If it's light enough for them to fight," said their editors remorselessly, "it's light enough for you to watch them." And out they had to go.

They had a perfectly miserable time. Edgar Wallace seems to have lost his way almost at once. He was found two days later in an almost starving condition at Steeple Bumpstead. How he got there nobody knows. He said he had set out to walk to where the noise of the guns seemed to be, and had gone on walking. Bennett Burleigh, that crafty old campaigner, had the sagacity to go by Tube. This brought him to Hampstead, the scene, it turned out later, of the fiercest operations, and with any luck he might have had a story to tell. But the lift stuck half-way up, owing to a German shell bursting in its neighbourhood, and it was not till the following evening that a search-party heard and rescued him.

The rest—A. G. Hales, Frederick Villiers, Charles Hands, and the others—met, on a smaller scale, the same fate as Edgar Wallace. Hales, starting for Tottenham, arrived in Croydon, very tired, with a nail in his boot. Villiers, equally unlucky, fetched up at Richmond. The most curious fate of all was reserved for Charles Hands. As far as can be gathered, he got on all right till he reached Leicester Square. There he lost his bearings, and seems to have walked round and round Shakespeare's statue, under the impression that he was going straight to Tottenham. After a day and a-half of this he sat down to rest, and was there found, when the fog had cleared, by a passing policeman.

And all the while the unseen guns boomed and thundered, and strange, thin shoutings came faintly through the darkness.

CHAPTER 10

THE TRIUMPH OF ENGLAND

It was the afternoon of Wednesday, September the Sixteenth. The battle had been over for twenty-four hours. The fog had thinned to a light lemon colour. It was raining.

By now the country was in possession of the main facts. Full details were not to be expected, though it is to the credit of the newspapers that, with keen enterprise, they had at once set to work to invent them, and on the whole had not done badly.

Broadly, the facts were that the Russian army, outmanoeuvered, had been practically annihilated. Of the vast force which had entered England with the other invaders there remained but a handful. These, the Grand Duke Vodkakoff among them, were prisoners in the German lines at Tottenham.

The victory had not been gained bloodlessly. Not a fifth of the German army remained. It is estimated that quite two-thirds of each army must have perished in that last charge of the Germans up the Hampstead heights, which ended in the storming of Jack Straw's Castle and the capture of the Russian general.

Prince Otto of Saxe-Pfennig lay sleeping in his tent at Tottenham. He was worn out. In addition to the strain of the battle, there had been the heavy work of seeing the interviewers, signing autograph-books, sitting to photographers, writing testimonials for patent medicines, and the thousand and one other tasks, burdensome but unavoidable, of the man who is in the public eye. Also he had caught a bad cold during the battle. A bottle of ammoniated quinine lay on the table beside him now as he slept.

As he lay there the flap of the tent was pulled softly aside. Two figures entered. Each was dressed in a flat-brimmed hat, a coloured handkerchief, a flannel shirt, football shorts, stockings, brown boots, and a whistle. Each carried a hockey-stick. One, however, wore spectacles and a look of quiet command which showed that he was the leader.

50

They stood looking at the prostrate general for some moments. Then the spectacled leader spoke.

"Scout-Master Wagstaff."

The other saluted.

"Wake him!"

Scout-Master Wagstaff walked to the side of the bed, and shook the sleeper's shoulder. The Prince grunted, and rolled over on to his other side. The Scout-Master shook him again. He sat up, blinking.

As his eyes fell on the quiet, stern, spectacled figure, he leaped from the bed.

"What—what—what," he stammered. "What's the beadig of this?"

He sneezed as he spoke, and, turning to the table, poured out and drained a bumper of ammoniated quinine.

"I told the sedtry pardicularly not to let adybody id. Who are you?"

The intruder smiled quietly.

"My name is Clarence Chugwater," he said simply.

"Jugwater? Dod't doe you frob Adab. What do you want? If you're forb sub paper, I cad't see you now. Cub to-borrow bordig."

"I am from no paper."

"Thed you're wud of these photographers. I tell you, I cad't see you."

"I am no photographer."

"Thed what are you?"

The other drew himself up.

"I am England," he said with a sublime gesture.

"Igglud! How do you bead you're Igglud? Talk seds."

Clarence silenced him with a frown.

"I say I am England. I am the Chief Scout, and the Scouts are England. Prince Otto, you thought this England of ours lay prone and helpless. You were wrong. The Boy Scouts were watching and waiting. And now their time has come. Scout-Master Wagstaff, do your duty."

The Scout-Master moved forward. The Prince, bounding to the bed, thrust his hand under the pillow. Clarence's voice rang out like a trumpet.

"Cover that man!"

The Prince looked up. Two feet away Scout-Master Wagstaff was standing, catapult in hand, ready to shoot.

"He is never known to miss," said Clarence warningly.

The Prince wavered.

51

"He has broken more windows than any other boy of his age in South London."

The Prince sullenly withdrew his hand—empty.

"Well, whad do you wad?" he snarled.

"Resistance is useless," said Clarence. "The moment I have plotted and planned for has come. Your troops, worn out with fighting, mere shadows of themselves, have fallen an easy prey. An hour ago your camp was silently surrounded by patrols of Boy Scouts, armed with catapults and hockey-sticks. One rush and the battle was over. Your entire army, like yourself, are prisoners."

"The diggids they are!" said the Prince blankly.

"England, my England!" cried Clarence, his face shining with a holy patriotism. "England, thou art free! Thou hast risen from the ashes of the dead self. Let the nations learn from this that it is when apparently crushed that the Briton is to more than ever be feared."

"Thad's bad grabbar," said the Prince critically.

"It isn't," said Clarence with warmth.

"It is, I tell you. Id's a splid idfididive."

Clarence's eyes flashed fire.

"I don't want any of your beastly cheek," he said. "Scout-Master Wagstaff, remove your prisoner."

"All the sabe," said the Prince, "id is a splid idfididive."

Clarence pointed silently to the door.

"And you doe id is," persisted the Prince. "And id's spoiled your big sbeech. Id—"

"Come on, can't you," interrupted Scout-Master Wagstaff.

"I ab cubbing, aren't I? I was odly saying—"

"I'll give you such a whack over the shin with this hockey-stick in a minute!" said the Scout-Master warningly. "Come on!"

The Prince went.

52

CHAPTER 11

CLARENCE—THE LAST PHASE

The brilliantly-lighted auditorium of the Palace Theatre.

Everywhere a murmur and stir. The orchestra is playing a selection. In the stalls fair women and brave men converse in excited whispers. One catches sentences here and there.

"Quite a boy, I believe!"

"How perfectly sweet!"

"'Pon honour, Lady Gussie, I couldn't say. Bertie Bertison, of the Bachelors', says a feller told him it was a clear thousand."

"Do you hear that? Mr. Bertison says that this boy is getting a thousand a week."

"Why, that's more than either of those horrid generals got."

"It's a lot of money, isn't it?"

"Of course, he did save the country, didn't he?"

"You may depend they wouldn't give it him if he wasn't worth it."

"Met him last night at the Duchess's hop. Seems a decent little chap. No side and that, if you know what I mean. Hullo, there's his number!"

The orchestra stops. The number 7 is displayed. A burst of applause, swelling into a roar as the curtain rises.

A stout man in crinkled evening-dress walks on to the stage.

"Ladies and gentlemen," he says, "I 'ave the 'onour to-night to introduce to you one whose name is, as the saying goes, a nouse'old word. It is thanks to 'im, to this 'ero whom I 'ave the 'onour to introduce to you to-night, that our beloved England no longer writhes beneath the ruthless 'eel of the alien oppressor. It was this 'ero's genius—and, I may say—er—I may say genius—that, unaided, 'it upon the only way for removing the cruel conqueror from our beloved 'earths and 'omes. It was this 'ero who, 'aving first allowed the invaders to claw each other to 'ash (if I may be permitted the expression) after the well-known precedent of the Kilkenny cats,

53

thereupon firmly and without flinching, stepped bravely in with his fellow-'eros—need I say I allude to our gallant Boy Scouts?—and dexterously gave what-for in no uncertain manner to the few survivors who remained."

Here the orator bowed, and took advantage of the applause to replenish his stock of breath. When his face had begun to lose the purple tinge, he raised his hand.

"I 'ave only to add," he resumed, "that this 'ero is engaged exclusively by the management of the Palace Theatre of Varieties, at a figure previously undreamed of in the annals of the music-hall stage. He is in receipt of the magnificent weekly salary of no less than one thousand one 'undred and fifty pounds a week."

Thunderous applause.

"I 'ave little more to add. This 'ero will first perform a few of those physical exercises which have made our Boy Scouts what they are, such as deep breathing, twisting the right leg firmly round the neck, and hopping on one foot across the stage. He will then give an exhibition of the various calls and cries of the Boy Scouts—all, as you doubtless know, skilful imitations of real living animals. In this connection I 'ave to assure you that he 'as nothing whatsoever in 'is mouth, as it 'as been sometimes suggested. In conclusion he will deliver a short address on the subject of 'is great exploits. Ladies and gentlemen, I have finished, and it only now remains for me to retire, 'aving duly announced to you England's Darling Son, the Country's 'Ero, the Nation's Proudest Possession—Clarence Chugwater."

A moment's breathless suspense, a crash from the orchestra, and the audience are standing on their seats, cheering, shouting, stamping.

A small sturdy, spectacled figure is on the stage.

It is Clarence, the Boy of Destiny.

A MAN OF MEANS

A SERIES OF SIX STORIES

THE EPISODE OF THE LANDLADY'S DAUGHTER

First of a Series of Six Stories [First published in Pictorial Review, May 1916]

When a seed-merchant of cautious disposition and an eye to the main chance receives from an eminent firm of jam-manufacturers an extremely large order for clover-seed, his emotions are mixed. Joy may be said to predominate, but with the joy comes also uncertainty. Are these people, he asks himself, proposing to set up as farmers of a large scale, or do they merely want the seed to give verisimilitude to their otherwise bald and unconvincing raspberry jam? On the solution of this problem depends the important matter of price, for, obviously, you can charge a fraudulent jam disseminator in a manner which an honest farmer would resent.

This was the problem which was furrowing the brow of Mr. Julian Fineberg, of Bury St. Edwards, one sunny morning when Roland Bleke knocked at his door; and such was its difficulty that only at the nineteenth knock did Mr. Fineberg raise his head.

"Come in—that dashed woodpecker out there!" he shouted, for it was his habit to express himself with a generous strength towards the junior members of his staff.

The young man who entered looked exactly like a second clerk in a provincial seed-merchant's office—which, strangely enough, he chanced to be. His chief characteristic was an intense ordinariness. He was a young man; and when you had said that of him you had

55

said everything. There was nothing which you would have noticed about him, except the fact that there was nothing to notice. His age was twenty-two and his name was Roland Bleke.

"Please, sir, it's about my salary."

Mr. Fineberg, at the word, drew himself together much as a British square at Waterloo must have drawn itself together at the sight of a squadron of cuirassiers.

"Salary?" he cried. "What about it? What's the matter with it? You get it, don't you?"

"Yes, sir, but——"

"Well? Don't stand there like an idiot. What is it?"

"It's too much."

Mr. Fineberg's brain reeled. It was improbable that the millennium could have arrived with a jerk; on the other hand, he had distinctly heard one of his clerks complain that his salary was too large. He pinched himself.

"Say that again," he said.

"If you could see your way to reduce it, sir——"

It occurred to Mr. Fineberg for one instant that his subordinate was endeavoring to be humorous, but a glance at Roland's face dispelled that idea.

"Why do you want it reduced?"

"Please, sir, I'm going to be married."

"What the deuce do you mean?"

"When my salary reaches a hundred and fifty, sir. And it's a hundred and forty now, so if you could see your way to knocking off ten pounds——"

Mr. Fineberg saw light. He was a married man himself.

"My boy," he said genially, "I quite understand. But I can do you better than that. It's no use doing this sort of thing in a small way. From now on your salary is a hundred and ten. No, no, don't thank me. You're an excellent clerk, and it's a pleasure to me to reward merit when I find it. Close the door after you."

And Mr. Fineberg returned with a lighter heart to the great clover-seed problem.

The circumstances which had led Roland to approach his employer may be briefly recounted. Since joining the staff of Mr. Fineberg, he had lodged at the house of a Mr. Coppin, in honorable employment as porter at the local railway-station. The Coppin family, excluding domestic pets, consisted of Mr. Coppin, a kindly and garrulous gentleman of sixty, Mrs. Coppin, a somewhat negative personality, most of whose life was devoted to cooking and washing up in her underground lair, Brothers Frank and Percy, gentleman of leisure, popularly supposed to be engaged in the mysterious occupation known as "lookin' about for somethin'," and, lastly, Muriel.

For some months after his arrival, Muriel had been to Roland Bleke a mere automaton, a something outside himself that was made only for neatly-laid breakfast tables and silent removal of plates at dinner. Gradually, however, when his natural shyness was soothed by use sufficiently to enable him to look at her when she came into the room, he discovered that she was a strikingly pretty girl, bounded to the North by a mass of auburn hair and to the South by small and shapely feet. She also possessed what, we are informed—we are children in these matters ourselves—is known as the R. S. V. P. eye. This eye had met Roland's one evening, as he chumped his chop, and before he knew what he was doing he had remarked that it had been a fine day.

From that wonderful moment matters had developed at an incredible speed. Roland had a nice sense of the social proprieties, and he could not bring himself to ignore a girl with whom he had once exchanged easy conversation about the weather. Whenever she came to lay his table, he felt bound to say something. Not being an experienced gagger, he found it more and more difficult each evening to hit on something bright, until finally, from sheer lack of inspiration, he kissed her.

If matters had progressed rapidly before, they went like lightning then. It was as if he had touched a spring or pressed a button, setting vast machinery in motion. Even as he reeled back stunned at his audacity, the room became suddenly full of Coppins of every variety known to science. Through a mist he was aware of Mrs. Coppin crying in a corner, of Mr. Coppin drinking his health in the remains of sparkling limado, of Brothers Frank and Percy, one on each side trying to borrow simultaneously half-crowns, and of Muriel, flushed but demure, making bread-pellets and throwing them in an abstracted way, one by one, at the Coppin cat, which had wandered in on the chance of fish.

Out of the chaos, as he stood looking at them with his mouth open, came the word "bans," and smote him like a blast of East wind.

It is not necessary to trace in detail Roland's mental processes from that moment till the day when he applied to Mr. Fineberg for a reduction of salary. It is enough to say that for quite a month he was extraordinarily happy. To a man who has had nothing to do with women, to be engaged is an intoxicating experience, and at first life was one long golden glow to Roland. Secretly, like all mild men, he had always nourished a desire to be esteemed a nut by his fellow men; and his engagement satisfied that desire. It was pleasant to hear Brothers Frank and Percy cough knowingly when he came in. It was pleasant to walk abroad with a girl like Muriel in the capacity of the accepted wooer. Above all, it was pleasant to sit holding Muriel's hand and watching the ill-concealed efforts of Mr. Albert Potter to hide his mortification. Albert was a mechanic in the motor-works round the corner, and hitherto Roland had always felt something of a worm in his presence. Albert was so infernally strong and silent and efficient. He could dissect a car and put it together again. He could drive through the thickest traffic. He could sit silent in company without having his silence attributed to shyness or imbecility. But—he could not get engaged to Muriel Coppin. That was reserved for Roland Bleke, the nut, the dasher, the young man of affairs. It was all very well being able to tell a spark-plug from a commutator at sight, but when it came to a contest in an affair of the heart with a man like Roland, Albert was in his proper place, third at the pole.

Probably, if he could have gone on merely being engaged, Roland would never have wearied of the experience. But the word marriage began to creep more and more into the family conversation, and suddenly panic descended upon Roland Bleke.

All his life he had had a horror of definite appointments. An invitation to tea a week ahead had been enough to poison life for him. He was one of those young men whose souls revolt at the thought of planning out any definite step. He could do things on the spur of the moment, but plans made him lose his nerve.

By the end of the month his whole being was crying out to him in agonized tones: "Get me out of this. Do anything you like, but get me out of this frightful marriage business."

If anything had been needed to emphasize his desire for freedom, the attitude of Frank and Percy would have supplied it. Every day they made it clearer that the man who married Muriel would be no stranger to them. It would be his pleasing task to support them, too, in the style to which they had become accustomed. They conveyed the idea that they went with Muriel as a sort of bonus.

The Coppin family were at high tea when Roland reached home. There was a general stir of interest as he entered the room, for it was known that he had left that morning with the intention of approaching Mr. Fineberg on the important matter of a rise in salary. Mr. Coppin removed his saucer of tea from his lips. Frank brushed the tail of a sardine from the corner of his mouth. Percy ate his haddock in an undertone. Albert Potter, who was present, glowered silently.

Roland shook his head with the nearest approach to gloom which his rejoicing heart would permit.

"I'm afraid I've bad news."

Mrs. Coppin burst into tears, her invariable practise in any crisis. Albert Potter's face relaxed into something resembling a smile.

"He won't give you your raise?"

Roland sighed.

"He's reduced me."

"Reduced you!"

"Yes. Times are bad just at present, so he has had to lower me to a hundred and ten."

The collected jaws of the family fell as one jaw. Muriel herself seemed to be bearing the blow with fortitude, but the rest were stunned. Frank and Percy might have been posing for a picture of men who had lost their fountain pens.

Beneath the table the hand of Albert Potter found the hand of Muriel Coppin, and held it; and Muriel, we regret to add, turned and bestowed upon Albert a half-smile of tender understanding.

"I suppose," said Roland, "we couldn't get married on a hundred and ten?"

"No," said Percy.

"No," said Frank.

"No," said Albert Potter.

They all spoke decidedly, but Albert the most decidedly of the three.

"Then," said Roland regretfully, "I'm afraid we must wait."

It seemed to be the general verdict that they must wait. Muriel said she thought they must wait. Albert Potter, whose opinion no one had asked, was quite certain that they must wait. Mrs. Coppin, between sobs, moaned that it would be best to wait. Frank and Percy, morosely devouring bread and jam, said they supposed they would have to wait. And, to end a painful scene, Roland drifted silently from the room, and went up-stairs to his own quarters.

There was a telegram on the mantel.

"Some fellows," he soliloquized happily, as he opened it, "wouldn't have been able to manage a little thing like that. They would have given themselves away. They would——"

The contents of the telegram demanded his attention.

For some time they conveyed nothing to him. The thing might have been written in Hindustani.

59

It would have been quite appropriate if it had been, for it was from the promoters of the Calcutta Sweep, and it informed him that, as the holder of ticket number 108,694, he had drawn Gelatine, and in recognition of this fact a check for five hundred pounds would be forwarded to him in due course.

Roland's first feeling was one of pure bewilderment. As far as he could recollect, he had never had any dealings whatsoever with these open-handed gentlemen. Then memory opened her flood-gates and swept him back to a morning ages ago, so it seemed to him, when Mr. Fineberg's eldest son Ralph, passing through the office on his way to borrow money from his father, had offered him for ten shillings down a piece of cardboard, at the same time saying something about a sweep. Partly from a vague desire to keep in with the Fineberg clan, but principally because it struck him as rather a doggish thing to do, Roland had passed over the ten shillings; and there, as far as he had known, the matter had ended.

And now, after all this time, that simple action had borne fruit in the shape of Gelatine and a check for five hundred pounds.

Roland's next emotion was triumph. The sudden entry of checks for five hundred pounds into a man's life is apt to produce this result.

For the space of some minutes he gloated; and then reaction set in. Five hundred pounds meant marriage with Muriel.

His brain worked quickly. He must conceal this thing. With trembling fingers he felt for his match-box, struck a match, and burnt the telegram to ashes. Then, feeling a little better, he sat down to think the whole matter over. His meditations brought a certain amount of balm. After all, he felt, the thing could quite easily be kept a secret. He would receive the check in due course, as stated, and he would bicycle over to the neighboring town of Lexingham and start a bank-account with it. Nobody would know, and life would go on as before.

He went to bed, and slept peacefully.

It was about a week after this that he was roused out of a deep sleep at eight o'clock in the morning to find his room full of Coppins. Mr. Coppin was there in a nightshirt and his official trousers. Mrs. Coppin was there, weeping softly in a brown dressing-gown. Modesty had apparently kept Muriel from the gathering, but brothers Frank and Percy stood at his bedside, shaking him by the shoulders and shouting. Mr. Coppin thrust a newspaper at him, as he sat up blinking.

These epic moments are best related swiftly. Roland took the paper, and the first thing that met his sleepy eye and effectually drove the sleep from it was this head-line:

And beneath it another in type almost as large as the first:

POOR CLERK WINS £40,000

His own name leaped at him from the printed page, and with it that of the faithful Gelatine.

Flight! That was the master-word which rang in Roland's brain as day followed day. The wild desire of the trapped animal to be anywhere except just where he was had come upon him. He was past the stage when conscience could have kept him to his obligations. He had ceased to think of anything or any one but himself. All he asked of Fate was to remove him from Bury St. Edwards on any terms.

It may be that some inkling of his state of mind was wafted telepathically to Frank and Percy, for it can not be denied that their behavior at this juncture was more than a little reminiscent of the police force. Perhaps it was simply their natural anxiety to keep an eye on what they already considered their own private gold-mine that made them so adhesive. Certainly there was no hour of the day when one or the other was not in Roland's immediate neighborhood. Their vigilance even extended to the night hours, and once, when Roland, having tossed sleeplessly on his bed, got up at two in the morning, with the wild idea of stealing out of the house and walking to London, a door opened as he reached the top of the stairs, and a voice asked him what he thought he was doing. The statement that he was walking in his sleep was accepted, but coldly.

It was shortly after this that, having by dint of extraordinary strategy eluded the brothers and reached the railway-station, Roland, with his ticket to London in his pocket and the express already entering the station, was engaged in conversation by old Mr. Coppin, who appeared from nowhere to denounce the high cost of living in a speech that lasted until the tail-lights of the train had vanished and Brothers Frank and Percy arrived, panting.

A man has only a certain capacity for battling with Fate. After this last episode Roland gave in. Not even the exquisite agony of hearing himself described in church as a bachelor of this parish, with the grim addition that this was for the second time of asking, could stir him to a fresh dash for liberty.

Altho the shadow of the future occupied Roland's mind almost to the exclusion of everything else, he was still capable of suffering a certain amount of additional torment from the present; and one of the things which made the present a source of misery to him was the fact that he was expected to behave more like a mad millionaire than a sober young man with a knowledge of the value of money. His mind, trained from infancy to a decent respect for the pence, had not yet adjusted itself to the possession of large means; and the open-handed role forced upon him by the family appalled him.

When the Coppins wanted anything, they asked for it; and it seemed to Roland that they wanted pretty nearly everything. If Mr. Coppin had reached his present age without the assistance of a gold watch, he might surely have struggled along to the end on gun-metal. In any case, a man of his years should have been thinking of higher things than mere gauds and trinkets. A like criticism applied to Mrs. Coppin's demand for a silk petticoat, which struck Roland as simply indecent. Frank and Percy took theirs mostly in specie. It was Muriel who struck the worst blow by insisting on a hired motor-car.

Roland hated motor-cars, especially when they were driven by Albert Potter, as this one was. Albert, that strong, silent man, had but one way of expressing his emotions, namely to open the throttle and shave the paint off trolley-cars. Disappointed love was giving Albert a good deal of discomfort at this time, and he found it made him feel better to go round corners on two wheels. As Muriel sat next to him on these expeditions, Roland squashing into the tonneau with Frank and Percy, his torments were subtle. He was not given a chance to forget, and the only way in which he could obtain a momentary diminution of the agony was to increase the speed to sixty miles an hour.

It was in this fashion that they journeyed to the neighboring town of Lexingham to see M. Etienne Feriaud perform his feat of looping the loop in his aeroplane.

It was Brother Frank's idea that they should make up a party to go and see M. Feriaud. Frank's was one of those generous, unspoiled natures which never grow blasé at the sight of a fellow human taking a sporting chance at hara-kiri. He was a well-known figure at every wild animal exhibition within a radius of fifty miles, and M. Feriaud drew him like a magnet.

"The blighter goes up," he explained, as he conducted the party into the arena, "and then he stands on his head and goes round in circles. I've seen pictures of it."

It appeared that M. Feriaud did even more than this. Posters round the ground advertised the fact that, on receipt of five pounds, he would take up a passenger with him. To date, however, there appeared to have been no rush on the part of the canny inhabitants of Lexingham to avail themselves of this chance of a breath of fresh

62

air. M. Feriaud, a small man with a chubby and amiable face, wandered about signing picture cards and smoking a lighted cigaret, looking a little disappointed.

Albert Potter was scornful.

"Lot of rabbits," he said. "Where's their pluck? And I suppose they call themselves Englishmen. I'd go up precious quick if I had a five-pound note. Disgrace, I call it, letting a Frenchman have the laugh of us."

It was a long speech for Mr. Potter, and it drew a look of respectful tenderness from Muriel. "You're so brave, Mr. Potter," she said.

Whether it was the slight emphasis which she put on the first word, or whether it was sheer generosity that impelled him, one can not say; but Roland produced the required sum even while she spoke. He offered it to his rival.

Mr. Potter started, turned a little pale, then drew himself up and waved the note aside.

"I take no favors," he said with dignity.

There was a pause.

"Why don't you do it." said Albert, nastily. "Five pounds is nothing to you."

"Why should I?"

"Ah! Why should you?"

It would be useless to assert that Mr. Potter's tone was friendly. It stung Roland. It seemed to him that Muriel was looking at him in an unpleasantly contemptuous manner.

In some curious fashion, without doing anything to merit it, he had apparently become an object of scorn and derision to the party.

"All right, then, I will," he said suddenly.

"Easy enough to talk," said Albert.

Roland strode with a pale but determined face to the spot where M. Feriaud, beaming politely, was signing a picture post-card.

Some feeling of compunction appeared to come to Muriel at the eleventh hour.

"Don't let him," she cried.

But Brother Frank was made of sterner stuff. This was precisely the sort of thing which, in his opinion, made for a jolly afternoon.

For years he had been waiting for something of this kind. He was experiencing that pleasant thrill which comes to a certain type

63

of person when the victim of a murder in the morning paper is an acquaintance of theirs.

"What are you talking about?" he said. "There's no danger. At least, not much. He might easily come down all right. Besides, he wants to. What do you want to go interfering for?"

Roland returned. The negotiations with the bird-man had lasted a little longer than one would have expected. But then, of course, M. Feriaud was a foreigner, and Roland's French was not fluent.

He took Muriel's hand.

"Good-by," he said.

He shook hands with the rest of the party, even with Albert Potter. It struck Frank that he was making too much fuss over a trifle—and, worse, delaying the start of the proceedings.

"What's it all about?" he demanded. "You go on as if we were never going to see you again."

"You never know."

"It's as safe as being in bed."

"But still, in case we never meet again——"

"Oh, well," said Brother Frank, and took the outstretched hand.

The little party stood and watched as the aeroplane moved swiftly along the ground, rose, and soared into the air. Higher and higher it rose, till the features of the two occupants were almost invisible.

"Now," said Brother Frank. "Now watch. Now he's going to loop the loop."

But the wheels of the aeroplane still pointed to the ground. It grew smaller and smaller. It was a mere speck.

"What the dickens?"

Far away to the West something showed up against the blue of the sky—something that might have been a bird, a toy kite, or an aeroplane traveling rapidly into the sunset.

Four pairs of eyes followed it in rapt silence.

THE EPISODE OF THE FINANCIAL NAPOLEON

Second of a Series of Six Stories [First published in Pictorial Review, June 1916]

Seated with his wife at breakfast on the veranda which overlooked the rolling lawns and leafy woods of his charming Sussex home, Geoffrey Windlebird, the great financier, was enjoying the morning sun to the full. His chubby features were relaxed in a smile of lazy contentment; and his wife, who liked to act sometimes as his secretary, found it difficult to get him to pay any attention to his morning's mail.

"There's a column in to-day's Financial Argus," she said, "of which you really must take notice. It's most abusive. It's about the Wildcat Reef. They assert that there never was any gold in the mine, and that you knew it when you floated the company."

"They will have their little joke."

"But you had the usual mining-expert's report."

"Of course we had. And a capital report it was. I remember thinking at the time what a neat turn of phrase the fellow had. I admit he depended rather on his fine optimism than on any examination of the mine. As a matter of fact, he never went near it. And why should he? It's down in South America somewhere. Awful climate—snakes, mosquitoes, revolutions, fever."

Mr. Windlebird spoke drowsily. His eyes closed.

"Well, the Argus people say that they have sent a man of their own out there to make inquiries, a well-known expert, and the report will be in within the next fortnight. They say they will publish it in their next number but one. What are you going to do about it?"

Mr. Windlebird yawned.

"Not to put too fine a point on it, dearest, the game is up. The Napoleon of Finance is about to meet his Waterloo. And all for twenty thousand pounds. That is the really bitter part of it. To-morrow we sail for the Argentine. I've got the tickets."

"You're joking, Geoffrey. You must be able to raise twenty thousand. It's a flea-bite."

65

"On paper—in the form of shares, script, bonds, promissory notes, it is a flea-bite. But when it has to be produced in the raw, in flat, hard lumps of gold or in crackling bank-notes, it's more like a bite from a hippopotamus. I can't raise it, and that's all about it. So—St. Helena for Napoleon."

Altho Geoffrey Windlebird described himself as a Napoleon of Finance, a Cinquevalli or Chung Ling Soo of Finance would have been a more accurate title. As a juggler with other people's money he was at the head of his class. And yet, when one came to examine it, his method was delightfully simple. Say, for instance, that the Home-grown Tobacco Trust, founded by Geoffrey in a moment of ennui, failed to yield those profits which the glowing prospectus had led the public to expect. Geoffrey would appease the excited shareholders by giving them Preference Shares (interest guaranteed) in the Sea-gold Extraction Company, hastily floated to meet the emergency. When the interest became due, it would, as likely as not, be paid out of the capital just subscribed for the King Solomon's Mines Exploitation Association, the little deficiency in the latter being replaced in its turn, when absolutely necessary and not a moment before, by the transfer of some portion of the capital just raised for yet another company. And so on, ad infinitum. There were moments when it seemed to Mr. Windlebird that he had solved the problem of Perpetual Promotion.

The only thing that can stop a triumphal progress like Mr. Windlebird's is when some coarse person refuses to play to the rules, and demands ready money instead of shares in the next venture. This had happened now, and it had flattened Mr. Windlebird like an avalanche.

He was a philosopher, but he could not help feeling a little galled that the demand which had destroyed him had been so trivial. He had handled millions—on paper, it was true, but still millions—and here he was knocked out of time by a paltry twenty thousand pounds.

"Are you absolutely sure that nothing can be done?" persisted Mrs. Windlebird. "Have you tried every one?"

"Every one, dear moon-of-my-delight—the probables, the possibles, the highly unlikelies, and the impossibles. Never an echo to the minstrel's wooing song. No, my dear, we have got to take to the boats this time. Unless, of course, some one possessed at one and the same time of twenty thousand pounds and a very confiding nature happens to drop from the clouds."

As he spoke, an aeroplane came sailing over the tops of the trees beyond the tennis-lawn. Gracefully as a bird it settled on the smooth turf, not twenty yards from where he was seated.

66

Roland Bleke stepped stiffly out onto the tennis-lawn. His progress rather resembled that of a landsman getting out of an open boat in which he has spent a long and perilous night at sea. He was feeling more wretched than he had ever felt in his life. He had a severe cold. He had a splitting headache. His hands and feet were frozen. His eyes smarted. He was hungry. He was thirsty. He hated cheerful M. Feriaud, who had hopped out and was now busy tinkering the engine, a gay Provencal air upon his lips, as he had rarely hated any one, even Muriel Coppin's brother Frank.

So absorbed was he in his troubles that he was not aware of Mr. Windlebird's approach until that pleasant, portly man's shadow fell on the turf before him.

"Not had an accident, I hope, Mr. Bleke?"

Roland was too far gone in misery to speculate as to how this genial stranger came to know his name. As a matter of fact, Mrs. Windlebird, keen student of the illustrated press, had recognized Roland by his photograph in the Daily Mirror. In the course of the twenty yards' walk from house to tennis-lawn she had put her husband into possession of the more salient points in Roland's history. It was when Mr. Windlebird heard that Roland had forty thousand pounds in the bank that he sat up and took notice.

"Lead me to him," he said simply.

Roland sneezed.

"Doe accident, thag you," he replied miserably. "Somethig's gone wrong with the worgs, but it's nothing serious, worse luck."

M. Feriaud, having by this time adjusted the defect in his engine, rose to his feet, and bowed.

"Excuse if we come down on your lawn. But not long do we trespass. See, mon ami," he said radiantly to Roland, "all now O. K. We go on."

"No," said Roland decidedly.

"No? What you mean—no?"

A shade of alarm fell on M. Feriaud's weather-beaten features. The eminent bird-man did not wish to part from Roland. Toward Roland he felt like a brother, for Roland had notions about payment for little aeroplane rides which bordered upon the princely.

"But you say—take me to France with you——"

"I know. But it's all off. I'm not feeling well."

"But it's all wrong." M. Feriaud gesticulated to drive home his point. "You give me one hundred pounds to take you away from Lexingham. Good. It is here." He slapped his breast pocket. "But the other two hundred pounds which also you promise me to pay me when I place you safe in France, where is that, my friend?"

67

"I will give you two hundred and fifty," said Roland earnestly, "to leave me here, and go right away, and never let me see your beastly machine again."

A smile of brotherly forgiveness lit up M. Feriaud's face. The generous Gallic nature asserted itself. He held out his arms affectionately to Roland.

"Ah, now you talk. Now you say something," he cried in his impetuous way. "Embrace me. You are all right."

Roland heaved a sigh of relief when, five minutes later, the aeroplane disappeared over the brow of the hill. Then he began to sneeze again.

"You're not well, you know," said Mr. Windlebird.

"I've caught cold. We've been flying about all night—that French ass lost his bearings—and my suit is thin. Can you direct me to a hotel?"

"Hotel? Nonsense." Mr. Windlebird spoke in the bluff, breezy voice which at many a stricken board-meeting had calmed frantic shareholders as if by magic. "You're coming right into my house and up to bed this instant."

It was not till he was between the sheets with a hot-water bottle at his toes and a huge breakfast inside him that Roland learned the name of his good Samaritan. When he did, his first impulse was to struggle out of bed and make his escape. Geoffrey Windlebird's was a name which he had learned, in the course of his mercantile career, to hold in something approaching reverence as that of one of the mightiest business brains of the age.

To have to meet so eminent a man in the capacity of invalid, a nuisance about the house, was almost too much for Roland's shrinking nature. The kindness of the Windlebirds—and there seemed to be nothing that they were not ready to do for him—distressed him beyond measure. To have a really great man like Geoffrey Windlebird sprawling genially over his bed, chatting away as if he were an ordinary friend, was almost horrible. Such condescension was too much.

Gradually, as he became convalescent, Roland found this feeling replaced by something more comfortable. They were such a genuine, simple, kindly couple, these Windlebirds, that he lost awe and retained only gratitude. He loved them both. He opened his heart to them. It was not long before he had told them the history of his career, skipping the earlier years and beginning with the entry of wealth into his life.

"It makes you feel funny," he confided to Mr. Windlebird's sympathetic ear, "suddenly coming into a pot of money like that.

68

You don't seem hardly able to realize it. I don't know what to do with it."

Mr. Windlebird smiled paternally.

"The advice of an older man who has had, if I may say so, some little experience of finance, might be useful to you there. Perhaps if you would allow me to recommend some sound investment——"

Roland glowed with gratitude.

"There's just one thing I'd like to do before I start putting my money into anything. It's like this."

He briefly related the story of his unfortunate affair with Muriel Coppin. Within an hour of his departure in the aeroplane, his conscience had begun to trouble him on this point. He felt that he had not acted well toward Muriel. True, he was practically certain that she didn't care a bit about him and was in love with Albert, the silent mechanic, but there was just the chance that she was mourning over his loss; and, anyhow, his conscience was sore.

"I'd like to give her something," he said. "How much do you think?"

Mr. Windlebird perpended.

"I'll tell you what I'll do. I'll send my own lawyer to her with— say, a thousand pounds—not a check, you understand, but one thousand golden sovereigns that he can show her—roll about on the table in front of her eyes. That'll console her. It's wonderful, the effect money in the raw has on people."

"I'd rather make it two thousand," said Roland. He had never really loved Muriel, and the idea of marrying her had been a nightmare to him; but he wanted to retreat with honor.

"Very well, make it two thousand, if you like. Tho I don't quite know how old Harrison is going to carry all that money."

As a matter of fact, old Harrison never had to try. On thinking it over, after he had cashed Roland's check, Mr. Windlebird came to the conclusion that seven hundred pounds would be quite as much money as it would be good for Miss Coppin to have all at once.

Mr. Windlebird's knowledge of human nature was not at fault. Muriel jumped at the money, and a letter in her handwriting informed Roland next morning that his slate was clean. His gratitude to Mr. Windlebird redoubled.

"And now," said Mr. Windlebird genially, "we can talk about that money of yours, and the best way of investing it. What you want is something which, without being in any way what is called speculative, nevertheless returns a fair and reasonable amount of interest. What you want is something sound, something solid, yet

69

something with a bit of a kick to it, something which can't go down and may go soaring like a rocket."

Roland quietly announced that was just what he did want, and lit another cigar.

"Now, look here, Bleke, my boy, as a general rule I don't give tips—But I've taken a great fancy to you, Bleke, and I'm going to break my rule. Put your money—" he sank his voice to a compelling whisper, "put every penny you can afford into Wildcat Reefs."

He leaned back with the benign air of the Alchemist who has just imparted to a favorite disciple the recently discovered secret of the philosopher's stone.

"Thank you very much, Mr. Windlebird," said Roland gratefully. "I will."

The Napoleonic features were lightened by that rare, indulgent smile.

"Not so fast, young man," laughed Mr. Windlebird. "Getting into Wildcat Reefs isn't quite so easy as you seem to think. Shall we say that you propose to invest thirty thousand pounds? Yes? Very well, then. Thirty thousand pounds! Why, if it got about that you were going to buy Wildcat Reefs on that scale the market would be convulsed."

Which was perfectly true. If it had got about that any one was going to invest thirty thousand pounds—or pence—in Wildcat Reefs, the market would certainly have been convulsed. The House would have rocked with laughter. Wildcat Reefs were a standing joke—except to the unfortunate few who still held any of the shares.

"The thing will have to be done very cautiously. No one must know. But I think—I say I think—I can manage it for you."

"You're awfully kind, Mr. Windlebird."

"Not at all, my dear boy, not at all. As a matter of fact, I shall be doing a very good turn to another pal of mine at the same time." He filled his glass. "This—" he paused to sip—"this pal of mine has a large holding of Wildcats. He wants to realize in order to put the money into something else, in which he is more personally interested." Mr. Windlebird paused. His mind dwelt for a moment on his overdrawn current account at the bank. "In which he is more personally interested," he repeated dreamily. "But of course you couldn't unload thirty pounds' worth of Wildcats in the public market."

"I quite see that," assented Roland.

"It might, however, be done by private negotiation," he said. "I must act very cautiously. Give me your check for the thirty thousand

70

to-night, and I will run up to town to-morrow morning, and see what I can do."

He did it. What hidden strings he pulled, what levers he used, Roland did not know. All Roland knew was that somehow, by some subtle means, Mr. Windlebird brought it off. Two days later his host handed him twenty thousand one-pound shares in the Wildcat Reef Gold-mine.

"There, my boy," he said.

"It's awfully kind of you, Mr. Windlebird."

"My dear boy, don't mention it. If you're satisfied, I'm sure I am."

Mr. Windlebird always spoke the truth when he could. He spoke it now.

It seemed to Roland, as the days went by, that nothing could mar the pleasant, easy course of life at the Windlebirds. The fine weather, the beautiful garden, the pleasant company—all these things combined to make this sojourn an epoch in his life.

He discovered his mistake one lovely afternoon as he sat smoking idly on the terrace. Mrs. Windlebird came to him, and a glance was enough to show Roland that something was seriously wrong. Her face was drawn and tired.

A moment before, Roland had been thinking life perfect. The only crumpled rose-leaf had been the absence of an evening paper. Mr. Windlebird would bring one back with him when he returned from the city, but Roland wanted one now. He was a great follower of county cricket, and he wanted to know how Surrey was faring against Yorkshire. But even this crumpled rose-leaf had been smoothed out, for Johnson, the groom, who happened to be riding into the nearest town on an errand, had promised to bring one back with him. He might appear at any moment now.

The sight of his hostess drove all thoughts of sport out of his mind. She was looking terribly troubled.

It flashed across Roland that both his host and hostess had been unusually silent at dinner the night before; and later, passing Mr. Windlebird's room on his way to bed, he had heard their voices, low and agitated. Could they have had some bad news?

"Mr. Bleke, I want to speak to you."

Roland moved like a sympathetic cow, and waited to hear more.

"You were not up when my husband left for the city this morning, or he would have told you himself. Mr. Bleke, I hardly know how to break it to you."

"Break it to me!"

71

"My husband advised you to put a very large sum of money in a mine called Wildcat Reefs."

"Yes. Thirty thousand pounds."

"As much as that! Oh, Mr. Bleke!"

She began to cry softly. She pressed his hand. Roland gaped at her.

"Mr. Bleke, there has been a terrible slump in Wildcat Reefs. To-day, they may be absolutely worthless."

Roland felt as if a cold hand had been laid on his spine.

"Wor-worthless!" he stammered.

Mrs. Windlebird looked at him with moist eyes.

"You can imagine how my husband feels about this. It was on his advice that you invested your money. He holds himself directly responsible. He is in a terrible state of mind. He is frantic. He has grown so fond of you, Mr. Bleke, that he can hardly face the thought that he has been the innocent instrument of your trouble."

Roland felt that it was an admirable comparison. His sensations were precisely those of a leading actor in an earthquake. The solid earth seemed to melt under him.

"We talked it over last night after you had gone to bed, and we came to the conclusion that there was only one honorable step to take. We must make good your losses. We must buy back those shares."

A ray of hope began to steal over Roland's horizon.

"But——" he began.

"There are no buts, really, Mr. Bleke. We should neither of us know a minute's peace if we didn't do it. Now, you paid thirty thousand pounds for the shares, you said? Well"—she held out a pink slip of paper to him—"this will make everything all right."

Roland looked at the check.

"But—but this is signed by you," he said.

"Yes. You see, if Geoffrey had to sign a check for that amount, it would mean selling out some of his stock, and in his position, with every movement watched by enemies, he can not afford to do it. It might ruin the plans of years. But I have some money of my own. My selling out stock doesn't matter, you see. I have post-dated the check a week, to give me time to realize on the securities in which my money is invested."

Roland's whole nature rose in revolt at this sacrifice. If it had been his host who had made this offer, he would have accepted it. But chivalry forbade his taking this money from a woman. A glow of self-sacrifice warmed him. After all, what was this money of his? He had never had any fun out of it. He had had so little acquaintance with it that for all practical purposes it might never have been his.

With a gesture which had once impressed him very favorably when exhibited on the stage by the hero of the number two company of "The Price of Honor," which had paid a six days' visit to Bury St. Edwards a few months before, he tore the check into little pieces.

"I couldn't accept it, Mrs. Windlebird," he said. "I can't tell you how deeply I appreciate your wonderful kindness, but I really couldn't. I bought the shares with my eyes open. The whole thing is nobody's fault, and I can't let you suffer for it. After the way you have treated me here, it would be impossible. I can't take your money. It's noble and generous of you in the extreme, but I can't accept it. I've still got a little money left, and I've always been used to working for my living, anyway, so—so it's all right."

"Mr. Bleke, I implore you."

Roland was hideously embarrassed. He looked right and left for a way of escape. He could hardly take to his heels, and yet there seemed no other way of ending the interview. Then, with a start of relief, he perceived Johnson the groom coming toward him with the evening paper.

"Johnson said he was going into the town," said Roland apologetically, "so I asked him to get me an evening paper. I wanted to see the lunch scores."

If he had been looking at his hostess then, an action which he was strenuously avoiding, he might have seen a curious spasm pass over her face. Mrs. Windlebird turned very pale and sat down suddenly in the chair which Roland had vacated at the beginning of their conversation. She lay back in it with her eyes closed. She looked tired and defeated.

Roland took the paper mechanically. He wanted it as a diversion to the conversation merely, for his interest in the doings of Surrey and Yorkshire had waned to the point of complete indifference in competition with Mrs. Windlebird's news.

Equally mechanically he unfolded it and glanced at front page; and, as he did do, a flaring explosion of headlines smote his eye.

Out of the explosion emerged the word "WILD-CATS".

"Why!" he exclaimed. "There's columns about Wild-cats on the front page here!"

"Yes?" Mrs. Windlebird's voice sounded strangely dull and toneless. Her eyes were still closed.

Roland took in the headlines with starting eyes.

73

THE WILD-CAT REEF GOLD-MINE
ANOTHER KLONDIKE
FRENZIED SCENES ON THE STOCK EXCHANGE
BROKERS FIGHT FOR SHARES
RECORD BOOM
UNPRECEDENTED RISE IN PRICES

Shorn of all superfluous adjectives and general journalistic exuberance, what the paper had to announce to its readers was this:

The "special commissioner" sent out by The Financial Argus to make an exhaustive examination of the Wild-cat Reef Mine—with the amiable view, no doubt, of exploding Mr. Geoffrey Windlebird once and for all with the confiding British public—has found, to his unbounded astonishment, that there are vast quantities of gold in the mine.

The discovery of the new reef, the largest and richest, it is stated, since the famous Mount Morgan, occurred with dramatic appropriateness on the very day of his arrival. We need scarcely remind our readers that, until that moment, Wild-cat Reef shares had reached a very low figure, and only a few optimists retained their faith in the mine. As the largest holder, Mr. Windlebird is to be heartily congratulated on this new addition to his fortune.

The publication of the expert's report in The Financial Argus has resulted in a boom in Wild-cats, the like of which can seldom have been seen on the Stock Exchange. From something like one shilling and sixpence per bundle the one pound shares have gone up to nearly
ten pounds a share, and even at this latter figure people were literally fighting to secure them.

The world swam about Roland. He was stupefied and even terrified. The very atmosphere seemed foggy. So far as his reeling brain was capable of thought, he figured that he was now worth about two hundred thousand pounds.

"Oh, Mrs. Windlebird," he cried, "It's all right after all."

Mrs. Windlebird sat back in her chair without answering.

"It's all right for every one," screamed Roland joyfully. "Why, if I've made a couple of hundred thousand, what must Mr.

Windlebird have netted. It says here that he is the largest holder. He must have pulled off the biggest thing of his life."

He thought for a moment.

"The chap I'm sorry for," he said meditatively, "is Mr. Windlebird's pal. You know. The fellow whom Mr. Windlebird persuaded to sell all his shares to me."

A faint moan escaped from his hostess's pale lips. Roland did not hear it. He was reading the cricket news.

THE EPISODE OF THE THEATRICAL VENTURE

Third of a Series of Six Stories [First published in Pictorial Review, July 1916]

It was one of those hard, nubbly rolls. The best restaurants charge you sixpence for having the good sense not to eat them. It hit Roland Bleke with considerable vehemence on the bridge of the nose. For the moment Roland fancied that the roof of the Regent Grill-room must have fallen in; and, as this would automatically put an end to the party, he was not altogether sorry. He had never been to a theatrical supper-party before, and within five minutes of his arrival at the present one he had become afflicted with an intense desire never to go to a theatrical supper-party again. To be a success at these gay gatherings one must possess dash; and Roland, whatever his other sterling qualities, was a little short of dash.

The young man on the other side of the table was quite nice about it. While not actually apologizing, he went so far as to explain that it was "old Gerry" whom he had had in his mind when he started the roll on its course. After a glance at old Gerry—a chinless child of about nineteen—Roland felt that it would be churlish to be angry with a young man whose intentions had been so wholly admirable. Old Gerry had one of those faces in which any alteration, even the comparatively limited one which a roll would be capable of producing, was bound to be for the better. He smiled a sickly smile and said that it didn't matter.

The charming creature who sat on his assailant's left, however, took a more serious view of the situation.

"Sidney, you make me tired," she said severely. "If I had thought you didn't know how to act like a gentleman I wouldn't have come here with you. Go away somewhere and throw bread at yourself, and ask Mr. Bleke to come and sit by me. I want to talk to him."

That was Roland's first introduction to Miss Billy Verepoint.

"I've been wanting to have a chat with you all the evening, Mr.

76

Bleke," she said, as Roland blushingly sank into the empty chair. "I've heard such a lot about you."

What Miss Verepoint had heard about Roland was that he had two hundred thousand pounds and apparently did not know what to do with it.

"In fact, if I hadn't been told that you would be here, I shouldn't have come to this party. Can't stand these gatherings of nuts in May as a general rule. They bore me stiff."

Roland hastily revised his first estimate of the theatrical profession. Shallow, empty-headed creatures some of them might be, no doubt, but there were exceptions. Here was a girl of real discernment—a thoughtful student of character—a girl who understood that a man might sit at a supper-party without uttering a word and might still be a man of parts.

"I'm afraid you'll think me very outspoken—but that's me all over. All my friends say, 'Billy Verepoint's a funny girl: if she likes any one she just tells them so straight out; and if she doesn't like any one she tells them straight out, too.'"

"And a very admirable trait," said Roland, enthusiastically.

Miss Verepoint sighed. "P'raps it is," she said pensively, "but I'm afraid it's what has kept me back in my profession. Managers don't like it: they think girls should be seen and not heard."

Roland's blood boiled. Managers were plainly a dastardly crew.

"But what's the good of worrying," went on Miss Verepoint, with a brave but hollow laugh. "Of course, it's wearing, having to wait when one has got as much ambition as I have; but they all tell me that my chance is bound to come some day."

The intense mournfulness of Miss Verepoint's expression seemed to indicate that she anticipated the arrival of the desired day not less than sixty years hence. Roland was profoundly moved. His chivalrous nature was up in arms. He fell to wondering if he could do anything to help this victim of managerial unfairness. "You don't mind my going on about my troubles, do you?" asked Miss Verepoint, solicitously. "One so seldom meets anybody really sympathetic."

Roland babbled fervent assurances, and she pressed his hand gratefully.

"I wonder if you would care to come to tea one afternoon," she said.

"Oh, rather!" said Roland. He would have liked to put it in a more polished way but he was almost beyond speech.

"Of course, I know what a busy man you are——"

77

"No, no!"

"Well, I should be in to-morrow afternoon, if you cared to look in."

Roland bleated gratefully.

"I'll write down the address for you," said Miss Verepoint, suddenly businesslike.

Exactly when he committed himself to the purchase of the Windsor Theater, Roland could never say. The idea seemed to come into existence fully-grown, without preliminary discussion. One moment it was not—the next it was. His recollections of the afternoon which he spent drinking lukewarm tea and punctuating Miss Verepoint's flow of speech with "yes's" and "no's" were always so thoroughly confused that he never knew even whose suggestion it was.

The purchase of a West-end theater, when one has the necessary cash, is not nearly such a complicated business as the layman might imagine. Roland was staggered by the rapidity with which the transaction was carried through. The theater was his before he had time to realize that he had never meant to buy the thing at all. He had gone into the offices of Mr. Montague with the intention of making an offer for the lease for, say, six months; and that wizard, in the space of less than an hour, had not only induced him to sign mysterious documents which made him sole proprietor of the house, but had left him with the feeling that he had done an extremely acute stroke of business. Mr. Montague had dabbled in many professions in his time, from street peddling upward, but what he was really best at was hypnotism.

Altho he felt, after the spell of Mr. Montague's magnetism was withdrawn, rather like a nervous man who has been given a large baby to hold by a strange woman who has promptly vanished round the corner, Roland was to some extent consoled by the praise bestowed upon him by Miss Verepoint. She said it was much better to buy a theater than to rent it, because then you escaped the heavy rent. It was specious, but Roland had a dim feeling that there was a flaw somewhere in the reasoning; and it was from this point that a shadow may be said to have fallen upon the brightness of the venture.

He would have been even less self-congratulatory if he had known the Windsor Theater's reputation. Being a comparative stranger in the metropolis, he was unaware that its nickname in theatrical circles was "The Mugs' Graveyard"—a title which had been bestowed upon it not without reason. Built originally by a slightly insane old gentleman, whose principal delusion was that the

78

public was pining for a constant supply of the Higher Drama, and more especially those specimens of the Higher Drama which flowed practically without cessation from the restless pen of the insane old gentleman himself, the Windsor Theater had passed from hand to hand with the agility of a gold watch in a gathering of race-course thieves. The one anxiety of the unhappy man who found himself, by some accident, in possession of the Windsor Theater, was to pass it on to somebody else. The only really permanent tenant it ever had was the representative of the Official Receiver.

Various causes were assigned for the phenomenal ill-luck of the theater, but undoubtedly the vital objection to it as a Temple of Drama lay in the fact that nobody could ever find the place where it was hidden. Cabmen shook their heads on the rare occasions when they were asked to take a fare there. Explorers to whom a stroll through the Australian bush was child's-play, had been known to spend an hour on its trail and finish up at the point where they had started.

It was precisely this quality of elusiveness which had first attracted Mr. Montague. He was a far-seeing man, and to him the topographical advantages of the theater were enormous. It was further from a fire-station than any other building of the same insurance value in London, even without having regard to the mystery which enveloped its whereabouts. Often after a good dinner he would lean comfortably back in his chair and see in the smoke of his cigar a vision of the Windsor Theater blazing merrily, while distracted firemen galloped madly all over London, vainly endeavoring to get some one to direct them to the scene of the conflagration. So Mr. Montague bought the theater for a mere song, and prepared to get busy.

Unluckily for him, the representatives of the various fire offices with which he had effected his policies got busy first. The generous fellows insisted upon taking off his shoulders the burden of maintaining the fireman whose permanent presence in a theater is required by law. Nothing would satisfy them but to install firemen of their own and pay their salaries. This, to a man in whom the instincts of the phoenix were so strongly developed as they were in Mr. Montague, was distinctly disconcerting. He saw himself making no profit on the deal—a thing which had never happened to him before.

And then Roland Bleke occurred, and Mr. Montague's belief that his race was really chosen was restored. He sold the Windsor Theater to Roland for twenty-five thousand pounds. It was fifteen thousand pounds more than he himself had given for it, and this very satisfactory profit mitigated the slight regret which he felt

79

when it came to transferring to Roland the insurance policies. To have effected policies amounting to rather more than seventy thousand pounds on a building so notoriously valueless as the Windsor Theater had been an achievement of which Mr. Montague was justly proud, and it seemed sad to him that so much earnest endeavor should be thrown away.

Over the little lunch with which she kindly allowed Roland to entertain her, to celebrate the purchase of the theater, Miss Verepoint outlined her policy.

"What we must put up at that theater," she announced, "is a revue. A revue," repeated Miss Verepoint, making, as she spoke, little calculations on the back of the menu, "we could run for about fifteen hundred a week—or, say, two thousand."

Saying two thousand, thought Roland to himself, is not quite the same as paying two thousand, so why should she stint herself?

"I know two boys who could write us a topping revue," said Miss Verepoint. "They'd spread themselves, too, if it was for me. They're in love with me—both of them. We'd better get in touch with them at once."

To Roland, there seemed to be something just the least bit sinister about the sound of that word "touch," but he said nothing.

"Why, there they are—lunching over there!" cried Miss Verepoint, pointing to a neighboring table. "Now, isn't that lucky?"

To Roland the luck was not quite so apparent, but he made no demur to Miss Verepoint's suggestion that they should be brought over to their table.

The two boys, as to whose capabilities to write a topping revue Miss Verepoint had formed so optimistic an estimate, proved to be well-grown lads of about forty-five and forty, respectively. Of the two, Roland thought that perhaps R. P. de Parys was a shade the more obnoxious, but a closer inspection left him with the feeling that these fine distinctions were a little unfair with men of such equal talents. Bromham Rhodes ran his friend so close that it was practically a dead heat. They were both fat and somewhat bulgy-eyed. This was due to the fact that what revue-writing exacts from its exponents is the constant assimilation of food and drink. Bromham Rhodes had the largest appetite in London; but, on the other hand, R. P. de Parys was a better drinker.

"Well, dear old thing!" said Bromham Rhodes.

"Well, old child!" said R. P. de Parys.

Both these remarks were addressed to Miss Verepoint. The talented pair appeared to be unaware of Roland's existence.

Miss Verepoint struck the business note. "Now you stop,

boys," she said. "Tie weights to yourselves and sink down into those chairs. I want you two lads to write a revue for me."

"Delighted!" said Bromham Rhodes; "but——"

"There is the trifling point to be raised first——" said R. P. de Parys.

"Where is the money coming from?" said Bromham Rhodes.

"My friend, Mr. Bleke, is putting up the money," said Miss Verepoint, with dignity. "He has taken the Windsor Theater."

The interest of the two authors in their host, till then languid, increased with a jerk. "Has he? By Jove!" they cried. "We must get together and talk this over."

It was Roland's first experience of a theatrical talking-over, and he never forgot it. Two such talkers-over as Bromham Rhodes and R. P. de Parys were scarcely to be found in the length and breadth of theatrical London. Nothing, it seemed, could the gifted pair even begin to think of doing without first discussing the proposition in all its aspects. The amount of food which Roland found himself compelled to absorb during the course of these debates was appalling. Discussions which began at lunch would be continued until it was time to order dinner; and then, as likely as not, they would have to sit there till supper-time in order to thrash the question thoroughly out.

The collection of a cast was a matter even more complicated than the actual composition of the revue. There was the almost insuperable difficulty that Miss Verepoint firmly vetoed every name suggested. It seemed practically impossible to find any man or woman in all England or America whose peculiar gifts or lack of them would not interfere with Miss Verepoint's giving a satisfactory performance of the principal role. It was all very perplexing to Roland; but as Miss Verepoint was an expert in theatrical matters, he scarcely felt entitled to question her views.

It was about this time that Roland proposed to Miss Verepoint. The passage of time and the strain of talking over the revue had to a certain extent moderated his original fervor. He had shaded off from a passionate devotion, through various diminishing tints of regard for her, into a sort of pale sunset glow of affection. His principal reason for proposing was that it seemed to him to be in the natural order of events. Her air towards him had become distinctly proprietorial. She now called him "Roly-poly" in public—a proceeding which left him with mixed feelings. Also, she had taken to ordering him about, which, as everybody knows, is an unmistakable sign of affection among ladies of the theatrical profession. Finally, in his chivalrous way, Roland had begun to feel a little apprehensive lest he might be compromising Miss Verepoint. Everybody knew that he was putting up the money for the revue in which she was to appear; they were constantly seen together at restaurants; people looked arch when they spoke to him about her. He had to ask himself: was he behaving like a perfect gentleman? The answer was in the negative. He took a cab to her flat and proposed before he could repent of his decision.

She accepted him. He was not certain for a moment whether he was glad or sorry. "But I don't want to get married," she went on, "until I have justified my choice of a profession. You will have to wait until I have made a success in this revue."

Roland was shocked to find himself hugely relieved at this concession.

The revue took shape. There did apparently exist a handful of artistes to whom Miss Verepoint had no objection, and these—a scrubby but confident lot—were promptly engaged. Sallow Americans sprang from nowhere with songs, dances, and ideas for effects. Tousled-haired scenic artists wandered in with model scenes under their arms. A great cloud of chorus-ladies settled upon the theater like flies. Even Bromham Rhodes and R. P. de Parys—those human pythons—showed signs of activity. They cornered Roland one day near Swan and Edgar's, steered him into the Piccadilly Grill-room and, over a hearty lunch, read him extracts from a brown-paper-covered manuscript which, they informed him, was the first act.

It looked a battered sort of manuscript and, indeed, it had every right to be. Under various titles and at various times, Bromham Rhodes' and R. P. de Parys' first act had been refused by practically every responsible manager in London. As "Oh! What a Life!" it had failed to satisfy the directors of the Empire. Re-christened "Wow-Wow!" it had been rejected by the Alhambra. The Hippodrome had refused to consider it, even under the name of "Hullo, Cellar-Flap!" It was now called, "Pass Along, Please!" and, according to its authors, was a real revue.

Roland was to learn, as the days went on, that in the world in which he was moving everything was real revue that was not a stunt or a corking effect. He floundered in a sea of real revue, stunts, and corking effects. As far as he could gather, the main difference between these things was that real revue was something which had been stolen from some previous English production, whereas a stunt or a corking effect was something which had been looted from New York. A judicious blend of these, he was given to understand, constituted the sort of thing the public wanted.

82

Rehearsals began before, in Roland's opinion, his little army was properly supplied with ammunition. True, they had the first act, but even the authors agreed that it wanted bringing up-to-date in parts. They explained that it was, in a manner of speaking, their life-work, that they had actually started it about ten years ago when they were careless lads. Inevitably, it was spotted here and there with smart topical hits of the early years of the century; but that, they said, would be all right. They could freshen it up in a couple of evenings; it was simply a matter of deleting allusions to pro-Boers and substituting lines about Marconi shares and mangel-wurzels. "It'll be all right," they assured Roland; "this is real revue."

In times of trouble there is always a point at which one may say, "Here is the beginning of the end." This point came with Roland at the commencement of the rehearsals. Till then he had not fully realized the terrible nature of the production for which he had made himself responsible. Moreover, it was rehearsals which gave him his first clear insight into the character of Miss Verepoint.

Miss Verepoint was not at her best at rehearsals. For the first time, as he watched her, Roland found himself feeling that there was a case to be made out for the managers who had so consistently kept her in the background. Miss Verepoint, to use the technical term, threw her weight about. There were not many good lines in the script of act one of "Pass Along, Please!" but such as there were she reached out for and grabbed away from their owners, who retired into corners, scowling and muttering, like dogs robbed of bones. She snubbed everybody, Roland included.

Roland sat in the cold darkness of the stalls and watched her, panic-stricken. Like an icy wave, it had swept over him what marriage with this girl would mean. He suddenly realised how essentially domestic his instincts really were. Life with Miss Verepoint would mean perpetual dinners at restaurants, bread-throwing suppers, motor-rides—everything that he hated most. Yet, as a man of honor, he was tied to her. If the revue was a success, she would marry him—and revues, he knew, were always successes. At that very moment there were six "best revues in London," running at various theaters. He shuddered at the thought that in a few weeks there would be seven.

He felt a longing for rural solitude. He wanted to be alone by himself for a day or two in a place where there were no papers with advertisements of revues, no grill-rooms, and, above all, no Miss Billy Verepoint. That night he stole away to a Norfolk village, where, in happier days, he had once spent a Summer holiday—a peaceful, primitive place where the inhabitants could not have told real revue from a corking effect.

Here, for the space of a week, Roland lay in hiding, while his quivering nerves gradually recovered tone. He returned to London happier, but a little apprehensive. Beyond a brief telegram of farewell, he had not communicated with Miss Verepoint for seven days, and experience had made him aware that she was a lady who demanded an adequate amount of attention.

That his nervous system was not wholly restored to health was borne in upon him as he walked along Piccadilly on his way to his flat; for, when somebody suddenly slapped him hard between the shoulder-blades, he uttered a stifled yell and leaped in the air.

Turning to face his assailant, he found himself meeting the genial gaze of Mr. Montague, his predecessor in the ownership of the Windsor Theater.

Mr. Montague was effusively friendly, and, for some mysterious reason, congratulatory.

"You've done it, have you? You pulled it off, did you? And in the first month—by George! And I took you for the plain, ordinary mug of commerce! My boy, you're as deep as they make 'em. Who'd have thought it, to look at you? It was the greatest idea any one ever had and staring me in the face all the time and I never saw it! But I don't grudge it to you—you deserve it my boy! You're a nut!"

"I really don't know what you mean."

"Quite right, my boy!" chuckled Mr. Montague. "You're quite right to keep it up, even among friends. It don't do to risk anything, and the least said soonest mended."

He went on his way, leaving Roland completely mystified.

Voices from his sitting-room, among which he recognized the high note of Miss Verepoint, reminded him of the ordeal before him. He entered with what he hoped was a careless ease of manner, but his heart was beating fast. Since the opening of rehearsals he had acquired a wholesome respect for Miss Verepoint's tongue. She was sitting in his favorite chair. There were also present Bromham Rhodes and R. P. de Parys, who had made themselves completely at home with a couple of his cigars and whisky from the oldest bin.

"So here you are at last!" said Miss Verepoint, querulously. "The valet told us you were expected back this morning, so we waited. Where on earth have you been to, running away like this, without a word?"

"I only went——"

"Well, it doesn't matter where you went. The main point is, what are you going to do about it?"

84

"We thought we'd better come along and talk it over," said R. P. de Parys.

"Talk what over?" said Roland: "the revue?"

"Oh, don't try and be funny, for goodness' sake!" snapped Miss Verepoint. "It doesn't suit you. You haven't the right shape of head. What do you suppose we want to talk over? The theater, of course."

"What about the theater?"

Miss Verepoint looked searchingly at him. "Don't you ever read the papers?"

"I haven't seen a paper since I went away."

"Well, better have it quick and not waste time breaking it gently," said Miss Verepoint. "The theater's been burned down— that's what's happened."

"Burned down?"

"Burned down!" repeated Roland.

"That's what I said, didn't I? The suffragettes did it. They left copies of 'Votes for Women' about the place. The silly asses set fire to two other theaters as well, but they happened to be in main thoroughfares and the fire-brigade got them under control at once. I suppose they couldn't find the Windsor. Anyhow, it's burned to the ground and what we want to know is what are you going to do about it?"

Roland was much too busy blessing the good angels of Kingsway to reply at once. R. P. de Parys, sympathetic soul, placed a wrong construction on his silence.

"Poor old Roly!" he said. "It's quite broken him up. The best thing we can do is all to go off and talk it over at the Savoy, over a bit of lunch."

"Well," said Miss Verepoint, "what are you going to do— rebuild the Windsor or try and get another theater?"

The authors were all for rebuilding the Windsor. True, it would take time, but it would be more satisfactory in every way. Besides, at this time of the year it would be no easy matter to secure another theater at a moment's notice.

To R. P. de Parys and Bromham Rhodes the destruction of the Windsor Theater had appeared less in the light of a disaster than as a direct intervention on the part of Providence. The completion of that tiresome second act, which had brooded over their lives like an ugly cloud, could now be postponed indefinitely.

"Of course," said R. P. de Parys, thoughtfully, "our contract with you makes it obligatory on you to produce our revue by a certain date—but I dare say, Bromham, we could meet Roly there, couldn't we?"

"Sure!" said Rhodes. "Something nominal, say a further five hundred on account of fees would satisfy us. I certainly think it would be better to rebuild the Windsor, don't you, R. P.?"

"I do," agreed R. P. de Parys, cordially. "You see, Roly, our revue has been written to fit the Windsor. It would be very difficult to alter it for production at another theater. Yes, I feel sure that rebuilding the Windsor would be your best course."

There was a pause.

"What do you think, Roly-poly?" asked Miss Verepoint, as Roland made no sign.

"Nothing would delight me more than to rebuild the Windsor, or to take another theater, or do anything else to oblige," he said, cheerfully. "Unfortunately, I have no more money to burn."

It was as if a bomb had suddenly exploded in the room. A dreadful silence fell upon his hearers. For the moment no one spoke. R. P. de Parys woke with a start out of a beautiful dream of prawn curry and Bromham Rhodes forgot that he had not tasted food for nearly two hours. Miss Verepoint was the first to break the silence.

"Do you mean to say," she gasped, "that you didn't insure the place?"

Roland shook his head. The particular form in which Miss Verepoint had put the question entitled him, he felt, to make this answer.

"Why didn't you?" Miss Verepoint's tone was almost menacing.

"Because it did not appear to me to be necessary."

Nor was it necessary, said Roland to his conscience. Mr. Montague had done all the insuring that was necessary—and a bit over.

Miss Verepoint fought with her growing indignation, and lost. "What about the salaries of the people who have been rehearsing all this time?" she demanded.

"I'm sorry that they should be out of an engagement, but it is scarcely my fault. However, I propose to give each of them a month's salary. I can manage that, I think."

Miss Verepoint rose. "And what about me? What about me, that's what I want to know. Where do I get off? If you think I'm going to marry you without your getting a theater and putting up this revue you're jolly well mistaken."

Roland made a gesture which was intended to convey regret and resignation. He even contrived to sigh.

86

"Very well, then," said Miss Verepoint, rightly interpreting this behavior as his final pronouncement on the situation. "Then everything's jolly well off."

She swept out of the room, the two authors following in her wake like porpoises behind a liner. Roland went to his bureau, unlocked it and took out a bundle of documents. He let his fingers stray lovingly among the fire insurance policies which energetic Mr. Montague had been at such pains to secure from so many companies.

"And so," he said softly to himself, "am I."

THE EPISODE OF THE LIVE WEEKLY

Fourth of a Series of Six Stories [First published in Pictorial Review, August 1916]

It was with a start that Roland Bleke realized that the girl at the other end of the bench was crying. For the last few minutes, as far as his preoccupation allowed him to notice them at all, he had been attributing the subdued sniffs to a summer cold, having just recovered from one himself.

He was embarrassed. He blamed the fate that had led him to this particular bench, but he wished to give himself up to quiet deliberation on the question of what on earth he was to do with two hundred and fifty thousand pounds, to which figure his fortune had now risen.

The sniffs continued. Roland's discomfort increased. Chivalry had always been his weakness. In the old days, on a hundred and forty pounds a year, he had had few opportunities of indulging himself in this direction; but now it seemed to him sometimes that the whole world was crying out for assistance.

Should he speak to her? He wanted to; but only a few days ago his eyes had been caught by the placard of a weekly paper bearing the title of 'Squibs,' on which in large letters was the legend "Men Who Speak to Girls," and he had gathered that the accompanying article was a denunciation rather than a eulogy of these individuals. On the other hand, she was obviously in distress.

Another sniff decided him.

"I say, you know," he said.

The girl looked at him. She was small, and at the present moment had that air of the floweret surprized while shrinking, which adds a good thirty-three per cent. to a girl's attractions. Her nose, he noted, was delicately tip-tilted. A certain pallor added to her beauty. Roland's heart executed the opening steps of a buck-and-wing dance.

"Pardon me," he went on, "but you appear to be in trouble. Is there anything I can do for you?"

88

She looked at him again—a keen look which seemed to get into Roland's soul and walk about it with a searchlight. Then, as if satisfied by the inspection, she spoke.

"No, I don't think there is," she said. "Unless you happen to be the proprietor of a weekly paper with a Woman's Page, and need an editress for it."

"I don't understand."

"Well, that's all any one could do for me—give me back my work or give me something else of the same sort."

"Oh, have you lost your job?"

"I have. So would you mind going away, because I want to go on crying, and I do it better alone. You won't mind my turning you out, I hope, but I was here first, and there are heaps of other benches."

"No, but wait a minute. I want to hear about this. I might be able—what I mean is—think of something. Tell me all about it."

There is no doubt that the possession of two hundred and fifty thousand pounds tones down a diffident man's diffidence. Roland began to feel almost masterful.

"Why should I?"

"Why shouldn't you?"

"There's something in that," said the girl reflectively. "After all, you might know somebody. Well, as you want to know, I have just been discharged from a paper called 'Squibs.' I used to edit the Woman's Page."

"By Jove, did you write that article on 'Men Who Speak——'?"

The hard manner in which she had wrapped herself as in a garment vanished instantly. Her eyes softened. She even blushed. Just a becoming pink, you know!

"You don't mean to say you read it? I didn't think that any one ever really read 'Squibs.'"

"Read it!" cried Roland, recklessly abandoning truth. "I should jolly well think so. I know it by heart. Do you mean to say that, after an article like that, they actually sacked you? Threw you out as a failure?"

"Oh, they didn't send me away for incompetence. It was simply because they couldn't afford to keep me on. Mr. Petheram was very nice about it."

"Who's Mr. Petheram?"

"Mr. Petheram's everything. He calls himself the editor, but he's really everything except office-boy, and I expect he'll be that next week. When I started with the paper, there was quite a large staff. But it got whittled down by degrees till there was only Mr. Petheram and myself. It was like the crew of the 'Nancy Bell.' They got eaten one by one, till I was the only one left. And now I've gone. Mr. Petheram is doing the whole paper now."

"How is it that he can't get anything better to do?" Roland said.

"He has done lots of better things. He used to be at Carmelite House, but they thought he was too old."

Roland felt relieved. He conjured up a picture of a white-haired elder with a fatherly manner.

"Oh, he's old, is he?"

"Twenty-four."

There was a brief silence. Something in the girl's expression stung Roland. She wore a rapt look, as if she were dreaming of the absent Petheram, confound him. He would show her that Petheram was not the only man worth looking rapt about.

He rose.

"Would you mind giving me your address?" he said.

"Why?"

"In order," said Roland carefully, "that I may offer you your former employment on 'Squibs.' I am going to buy it."

After all, your man of dash and enterprise, your Napoleon, does have his moments. Without looking at her, he perceived that he had bowled her over completely. Something told him that she was staring at him, open-mouthed. Meanwhile, a voice within him was muttering anxiously, "I wonder how much this is going to cost."

"You're going to buy 'Squibs!'"

Her voice had fallen away to an awestruck whisper.

"I am."

She gulped.

"Well, I think you're wonderful."

So did Roland.

"Where will a letter find you?" he asked.

"My name is March. Bessie March. I'm living at twenty-seven Guildford Street."

"Twenty-seven. Thank you. Good morning. I will communicate with you in due course."

He raised his hat and walked away. He had only gone a few steps, when there was a patter of feet behind him. He turned.

"I—I just wanted to thank you," she said.

"Not at all," said Roland. "Not at all."

He went on his way, tingling with just triumph. Petheram? Who was Petheram? Who, in the name of goodness, was Petheram? He had put Petheram in his proper place, he rather fancied. Petheram, forsooth. Laughable.

A copy of the current number of 'Squibs,' purchased at a book-stall, informed him, after a minute search to find the editorial page, that the offices of the paper were in Fetter Lane. It was evidence of his exalted state of mind that he proceeded thither in a cab.

Fetter Lane is one of those streets in which rooms that have only just escaped being cupboards by a few feet achieve the dignity of offices. There might have been space to swing a cat in the editorial sanctum of 'Squibs,' but it would have been a near thing. As for the outer office, in which a vacant-faced lad of fifteen received Roland and instructed him to wait while he took his card in to Mr. Petheram, it was a mere box. Roland was afraid to expand his chest for fear of bruising it.

The boy returned to say that Mr. Petheram would see him.

Mr. Petheram was a young man with a mop of hair, and an air of almost painful restraint. He was in his shirt-sleeves, and the table before him was heaped high with papers. Opposite him, evidently in the act of taking his leave was a comfortable-looking man of middle age with a red face and a short beard. He left as Roland entered and Roland was surprized to see Mr. Petheram spring to his feet, shake his fist at the closing door, and kick the wall with a vehemence which brought down several inches of discolored plaster.

"Take a seat," he said, when he had finished this performance. "What can I do for you?"

Roland had always imagined that editors in their private offices were less easily approached and, when approached, more brusk. The fact was that Mr. Petheram, whose optimism nothing could quench, had mistaken him for a prospective advertiser.

"I want to buy the paper," said Roland. He was aware that this was an abrupt way of approaching the subject, but, after all, he did want to buy the paper, so why not say so?

Mr. Petheram fizzed in his chair. He glowed with excitement.

"Do you mean to tell me there's a single book-stall in London which has sold out? Great Scott, perhaps they've all sold out! How many did you try?"

"I mean buy the whole paper. Become proprietor, you know."

Roland felt that he was blushing, and hated himself for it. He ought to be carrying this thing through with an air. Mr. Petheram looked at him blankly.

"Why?" he asked.

"Oh, I don't know," said Roland. He felt the interview was going all wrong. It lacked a stateliness which this kind of interview should have had.

"Honestly?" said Mr. Petheram. "You aren't pulling my leg?"

91

Roland nodded. Mr. Petheram appeared to struggle with his conscience, and finally to be worsted by it, for his next remarks were limpidly honest.

"Don't you be an ass," he said. "You don't know what you're letting yourself in for. Did you see that blighter who went out just now? Do you know who he is? That's the fellow we've got to pay five pounds a week to for life."

"Why?"

"We can't get rid of him. When the paper started, the proprietors—not the present ones—thought it would give the thing a boom if they had a football competition with a first prize of a fiver a week for life. Well, that's the man who won it. He's been handed down as a legacy from proprietor to proprietor, till now we've got him. Ages ago they tried to get him to compromise for a lump sum down, but he wouldn't. Said he would only spend it, and preferred to get it by the week. Well, by the time we've paid that vampire, there isn't much left out of our profits. That's why we are at the present moment a little understaffed."

A frown clouded Mr. Petheram's brow. Roland wondered if he was thinking of Bessie March.

"I know all about that," he said.

"And you still want to buy the thing?"

"Yes."

"But what on earth for? Mind you, I ought not to be crabbing my own paper like this, but you seem a good chap, and I don't want to see you landed. Why are you doing it?"

"Oh, just for fun."

"Ah, now you're talking. If you can afford expensive amusements, go ahead."

He put his feet on the table, and lit a short pipe. His gloomy views on the subject of 'Squibs' gave way to a wave of optimism.

"You know," he said, "there's really a lot of life in the old rag yet. If it were properly run. What has hampered us has been lack of capital. We haven't been able to advertise. I'm bursting with ideas for booming the paper, only naturally you can't do it for nothing. As for editing, what I don't know about editing—but perhaps you had got somebody else in your mind?"

"No, no," said Roland, who would not have known an editor from an office-boy. The thought of interviewing prospective editors appalled him.

"Very well, then," resumed Mr. Petheram, reassured, kicking over a heap of papers to give more room for his feet. "Take it that I continue as editor. We can discuss terms later. Under the present regime I have been doing all the work in exchange for a happy home. I suppose you won't want to spoil the ship for a ha'porth of tar? In other words, you would sooner have a happy, well-fed editor running about the place than a broken-down wreck who might swoon from starvation?"

"But one moment," said Roland. "Are you sure that the present proprietors will want to sell?"

"Want to sell," cried Mr. Petheram enthusiastically. "Why, if they know you want to buy, you've as much chance of getting away from them without the paper as—as—well, I can't think of anything that has such a poor chance of anything. If you aren't quick on your feet, they'll cry on your shoulder. Come along, and we'll round them up now."

He struggled into his coat, and gave his hair an impatient brush with a note-book.

"There's just one other thing," said Roland. "I have been a regular reader of 'Squibs' for some time, and I particularly admire the way in which the Woman's Page——"

"You mean you want to reengage the editress? Rather. You couldn't do better. I was going to suggest it myself. Now, come along quick before you change your mind or wake up."

Within a very few days of becoming sole proprietor of 'Squibs,' Roland began to feel much as a man might who, a novice at the art of steering cars, should find himself at the wheel of a runaway motor. Young Mr. Petheram had spoken nothing less than the truth when he had said that he was full of ideas for booming the paper. The infusion of capital into the business acted on him like a powerful stimulant. He exuded ideas at every pore.

Roland's first notion had been to engage a staff of contributors. He was under the impression that contributors were the life-blood of a weekly journal. Mr. Petheram corrected this view. He consented to the purchase of a lurid serial story, but that was the last concession he made. Nobody could accuse Mr. Petheram of lack of energy. He was willing, even anxious, to write the whole paper himself, with the exception of the Woman's Page, now brightly conducted once more by Miss March. What he wanted Roland to concentrate himself upon was the supplying of capital for ingenious advertising schemes.

"How would it be," he asked one morning—he always began his remarks with, "How would it be?"—"if we paid a man to walk down Piccadilly in white skin-tights with the word 'Squibs' painted in red letters across his chest?"

Roland thought it would certainly not be.

"Good sound advertising stunt," urged Mr. Petheram. "You

don't like it? All right. You're the boss. Well, how would it be to have a squad of men dressed as Zulus with white shields bearing the legend 'Squibs?' See what I mean? Have them sprinting along the Strand shouting, 'Wah! Wah! Wah! Buy it! Buy it!' It would make people talk."

Roland emerged from these interviews with his skin crawling with modest apprehension. His was a retiring nature, and the thought of Zulus sprinting down the Strand shouting "Wah! Wah! Wah! Buy it! Buy it!" with reference to his personal property appalled him.

He was beginning now heartily to regret having bought the paper, as he generally regretted every definite step which he took. The glow of romance which had sustained him during the preliminary negotiations had faded entirely. A girl has to be possessed of unusual charm to continue to captivate B, when she makes it plain daily that her heart is the exclusive property of A; and Roland had long since ceased to cherish any delusion that Bessie March was ever likely to feel anything but a mild liking for him. Young Mr. Petheram had obviously staked out an indisputable claim. Her attitude toward him was that of an affectionate devotee toward a high priest. One morning, entering the office unexpectedly, Roland found her kissing the top of Mr. Petheram's head; and from that moment his interest in the fortunes of 'Squibs' sank to zero. It amazed him that he could ever have been idiot enough to have allowed himself to be entangled in this insane venture for the sake of an insignificant-looking bit of a girl with a snub-nose and a poor complexion.

What particularly galled him was the fact that he was throwing away good cash for nothing. It was true that his capital was more than equal to the, on the whole, modest demands of the paper, but that did not alter the fact that he was wasting money. Mr. Petheram always talked buoyantly about turning the corner, but the corner always seemed just as far off.

The old idea of flight, to which he invariably had recourse in any crisis, came upon Roland with irresistible force. He packed a bag, and went to Paris. There, in the discomforts of life in a foreign country, he contrived for a month to forget his white elephant.

He returned by the evening train which deposits the traveler in London in time for dinner.

Strangely enough, nothing was farther from Roland's mind than his bright weekly paper, as he sat down to dine in a crowded grill-room near Piccadilly Circus. Four weeks of acute torment in a city where nobody seemed to understand the simplest English

94

sentence had driven 'Squibs' completely from his mind for the time being.

The fact that such a paper existed was brought home to him with the coffee. A note was placed upon his table by the attentive waiter.

"What's this?" he asked.

"The lady, sare," said the waiter vaguely.

Roland looked round the room excitedly. The spirit of romance gripped him. There were many ladies present, for this particular restaurant was a favorite with artistes who were permitted to "look in" at their theaters as late as eight-thirty. None of them looked particularly self-conscious, yet one of them had sent him this quite unsolicited tribute. He tore open the envelope.

The message, written in a flowing feminine hand, was brief, and Mrs. Grundy herself could have taken no exception to it.

"'Squibs,' one penny weekly, buy it," it ran. All the mellowing effects of a good dinner passed away from Roland. He was feverishly irritated. He paid his bill and left the place.

A visit to a neighboring music-hall occurred to him as a suitable sedative. Hardly had his nerves ceased to quiver sufficiently to allow him to begin to enjoy the performance, when, in the interval between two of the turns, a man rose in one of the side boxes.

"Is there a doctor in the house?"

There was a hush in the audience. All eyes were directed toward the box. A man in the stalls rose, blushing, and cleared his throat.

"My wife has fainted," continued the speaker. "She has just discovered that she has lost her copy of 'Squibs.'"

The audience received the statement with the bovine stolidity of an English audience in the presence of the unusual.

Not so Roland. Even as the purposeful-looking chuckers-out wended their leopard-like steps toward the box, he was rushing out into the street.

As he stood cooling his indignation in the pleasant breeze which had sprung up, he was aware of a dense crowd proceeding toward him. It was headed by an individual who shone out against the drab background like a good deed in a naughty world. Nature hath framed strange fellows in her time, and this was one of the strangest that Roland's bulging eyes had ever rested upon. He was a large, stout man, comfortably clad in a suit of white linen, relieved by a scarlet 'Squibs' across the bosom. His top-hat, at least four sizes larger than any top-hat worn out of a pantomime, flaunted the same word in letters of flame. His umbrella, which, tho the weather was fine, he carried open above his head, bore the device "One penny weekly".

The arrest of this person by a vigilant policeman and Roland's dive into a taxicab occurred simultaneously. Roland was blushing all over. His head was in a whirl. He took the evening paper handed in through the window of the cab quite mechanically, and it was only the strong exhortations of the vendor which eventually induced him to pay for it. This he did with a sovereign, and the cab drove off.

He was just thinking of going to bed several hours later, when it occurred to him that he had not read his paper. He glanced at the first page. The middle column was devoted to a really capitally written account of the proceedings at Bow Street consequent upon the arrest of six men who, it was alleged, had caused a crowd to collect to the disturbance of the peace by parading the Strand in the undress of Zulu warriors, shouting in unison the words "Wah! Wah! Wah! Buy 'Squibs.'"

Young Mr. Petheram greeted Roland with a joyous enthusiasm which the hound Argus, on the return of Ulysses, might have equalled but could scarcely have surpassed.

It seemed to be Mr. Petheram's considered opinion that God was in His Heaven and all was right with the world. Roland's attempts to correct this belief fell on deaf ears.

"Have I seen the advertisements?" he cried, echoing his editor's first question. "I've seen nothing else."

"There!" said Mr. Petheram proudly.

"It can't go on."

"Yes, it can. Don't you worry. I know they're arrested as fast as we send them out, but, bless you, the supply's endless. Ever since the Revue boom started and actors were expected to do six different parts in seven minutes, there are platoons of music-hall 'pros' hanging about the Strand, ready to take on any sort of job you offer them. I have a special staff flushing the Bodegas. These fellows love it. It's meat and drink to them to be right in the public eye like that. Makes them feel ten years younger. It's wonderful the talent knocking about. Those Zulus used to have a steady job as the Six Brothers Biff, Society Contortionists. The Revue craze killed them professionally. They cried like children when we took them on.

"By the way, could you put through an expenses cheque before you go? The fines mount up a bit. But don't you worry about that either. We're coining money. I'll show you the returns in a minute. I told you we should turn the corner. Turned it! Blame me, we've whizzed round it on two wheels. Have you had time to see the paper since you got back? No? Then you haven't seen our new Scandal Page—'We Just Want to Know, You Know.' It's a corker, and it's sent the circulation up like a rocket. Everybody reads 'Squibs' now. I was hoping you would come back soon. I wanted to ask you about taking new offices. We're a bit above this sort of thing now."

Roland, meanwhile, was reading with horrified eyes the alleged corking Scandal Page. It seemed to him without exception the most frightful production he had ever seen. It appalled him.

"This is awful," he moaned. "We shall have a hundred libel actions."

"Oh, no, that's all right. It's all fake stuff, tho the public doesn't know it. If you stuck to real scandals you wouldn't get a par. a week. A more moral set of blameless wasters than the blighters who constitute modern society you never struck. But it reads all right, doesn't it? Of course, every now and then one does hear something genuine, and then it goes in. For instance, have you ever heard of Percy Pook, the bookie? I have got a real ripe thing in about Percy this week, the absolute limpid truth. It will make him sit up a bit. There, just under your thumb."

Roland removed his thumb, and, having read the paragraph in question, started as if he had removed it from a snake.

"But this is bound to mean a libel action!" he cried.

"Not a bit of it," said Mr. Petheram comfortably. "You don't know Percy. I won't bore you with his life-history, but take it from me he doesn't rush into a court of law from sheer love of it. You're safe enough."

But it appeared that Mr. Pook, tho coy in the matter of cleansing his scutcheon before a judge and jury, was not wholly without weapons of defense and offense. Arriving at the office next day, Roland found a scene of desolation, in the middle of which, like Marius among the ruins of Carthage, sat Jimmy, the vacant-faced office boy. Jimmy was reading an illustrated comic paper, and appeared undisturbed by his surroundings.

"He's gorn," he observed, looking up as Roland entered.

"What do you mean?" Roland snapped at him. "Who's gone and where did he go? And besides that, when you speak to your superiors you will rise and stop chewing that infernal gum. It gets on my nerves."

Jimmy neither rose nor relinquished his gum. He took his time and answered.

"Mr. Petheram. A couple of fellers come in and went through, and there was a uproar inside there, and presently out they come running, and I went in, and there was Mr. Petheram on the floor

97

knocked silly and the furniture all broke, and now 'e's gorn to 'orspital. Those fellers 'ad been putting 'im froo it proper," concluded Jimmy with moody relish.

Roland sat down weakly. Jimmy, his tale told, resumed the study of his illustrated paper. Silence reigned in the offices of 'Squibs.'

It was broken by the arrival of Miss March. Her exclamation of astonishment at the sight of the wrecked room led to a repetition of Jimmy's story.

She vanished on hearing the name of the hospital to which the stricken editor had been removed, and returned an hour later with flashing eyes and a set jaw.

"Aubrey," she said—it was news to Roland that Mr. Petheram's name was Aubrey—"is very much knocked about, but he is conscious and sitting up and taking nourishment."

"That's good."

"In a spoon only."

"Ah!" said Roland.

"The doctor says he will not be out for a week. Aubrey is certain it was that horrible book-maker's men who did it, but of course he can prove nothing. But his last words to me were, 'Slip it into Percy again this week.' He has given me one or two things to mention. I don't understand them, but Aubrey says they will make him wild."

Roland's flesh crept. The idea of making Mr. Pook any wilder than he appeared to be at present horrified him. Panic gave him strength, and he addressed Miss March, who was looking more like a modern Joan of Arc than anything else on earth, firmly.

"Miss March," he said, "I realize that this is a crisis, and that we must all do all that we can for the paper, and I am ready to do anything in reason—but I will not slip it into Percy. You have seen the effects of slipping it into Percy. What he or his minions will do if we repeat the process I do not care to think."

"You are afraid?"

"Yes," said Roland simply.

Miss March turned on her heel. It was plain that she regarded him as a worm. Roland did not like being thought a worm, but it was infinitely better than being regarded as an interesting case by the house-surgeon of a hospital. He belonged to the school of thought which holds that it is better that people should say of you, "There he goes!" than that they should say, "How peaceful he looks".

Stress of work prevented further conversation. It was a revelation to Roland, the vigor and energy with which Miss March threw herself into the breach. As a matter of fact, so tremendous had been the labors of the departed Mr. Petheram, that her work was more apparent than real. Thanks to Mr. Petheram, there was a sufficient supply of material in hand to enable 'Squibs' to run a fortnight on its own momentum. Roland, however, did not know this, and with a view to doing what little he could to help, he informed Miss March that he would write the Scandal Page. It must be added that the offer was due quite as much to prudence as to chivalry. Roland simply did not dare to trust her with the Scandal Page. In her present mood it was not safe. To slip it into Percy would, he felt, be with her the work of a moment.

Literary composition had never been Roland's forte. He sat and stared at the white paper and chewed the pencil which should have been marring its whiteness with stinging paragraphs. No sort of idea came to him.

His brow grew damp. What sort of people—except book-makers—did things you could write scandal about? As far as he could ascertain, nobody.

He picked up the morning paper. The name Windlebird[1] caught his eye. A kind of pleasant melancholy came over him as he read the paragraph. How long ago it seemed since he had met that genial financier. The paragraph was not particularly interesting. It gave a brief account of some large deal which Mr. Windlebird was negotiating. Roland did not understand a word of it, but it gave him an idea.

Mr. Windlebird's financial standing, he knew, was above suspicion. Mr. Windlebird had made that clear to him during his visit. There could be no possibility of offending Mr. Windlebird by a paragraph or two about the manners and customs of financiers. Phrases which his kindly host had used during his visit came back to him, and with them inspiration.

Within five minutes he had compiled the following

WE JUST WANT TO KNOW, YOU KNOW

WHO is the eminent financier at present engaged upon one of his biggest deals?

WHETHER the public would not be well-advised to look a little closer into it before investing their money?

---

[1] He is a character in the Second Episode, a fraudulent financier.

IF it is not a fact that this gentleman has bought a first-class ticket to the Argentine in case of accidents?

WHETHER he may not have to use it at any moment?

After that it was easy. Ideas came with a rush. By the end of an hour he had completed a Scandal Page of which Mr. Petheram himself might have been proud, without a suggestion of slipping it into Percy. He felt that he could go to Mr. Pook, and say, "Percy, on your honor as a British book-maker, have I slipped it into you in any way whatsoever?" And Mr. Pook would be compelled to reply, "You have not."

Miss March read the proofs of the page, and sniffed. But Miss March's blood was up, and she would have sniffed at anything not directly hostile to Mr. Pook.

A week later Roland sat in the office of 'Squibs,' reading a letter. It had been sent from No. 18-A Bream's Buildings, E.C., but, from Roland's point of view, it might have come direct from heaven; for its contents, signed by Harrison, Harrison, Harrison & Harrison, Solicitors, were to the effect that a client of theirs had instructed them to approach him with a view to purchasing the paper. He would not find their client disposed to haggle over terms, so, hoped Messrs. Harrison, Harrison, Harrison & Harrison, in the event of Roland being willing to sell, they could speedily bring matters to a satisfactory conclusion.

Any conclusion which had left him free of 'Squibs' without actual pecuniary loss would have been satisfactory to Roland. He had conceived a loathing for his property which not even its steadily increasing sales could mitigate. He was around at Messrs. Harrison's office as soon as a swift taxi could take him there. The lawyers were for spinning the thing out with guarded remarks and cautious preambles, but Roland's methods of doing business were always rapid.

"This chap," he said, "this fellow who wants to buy 'Squibs,' what'll he give?"

"That," began one of the Harrisons ponderously, "would, of course, largely depend——"

"I'll take five thousand. Lock, stock, and barrel, including the present staff, an even five thousand. How's that?"

"Five thousand is a large——"

"Take it or leave it."

"My dear sir, you hold a pistol to our heads. However, I think that our client might consent to the sum you mention."

100

"Good. Well, directly I get his check, the thing's his. By the way, who is your client?"

Mr. Harrison coughed.

"His name," he said, "will be familiar to you. He is the eminent financier, Mr. Geoffrey Windlebird."

THE DIVERTING EPISODE OF THE EXILED MONARCH

Fifth of a Series of Six Stories [First published in Pictorial Review, September 1916]

The caoutchouc was drawing all London. Slightly more indecent than the Salome dance, a shade less reticent than ragtime, it had driven the tango out of existence. Nor, indeed, did anybody actually caoutchouc, for the national dance of Paranoya contained three hundred and fifteen recognized steps; but everybody tried to. A new revue, "Hullo, Caoutchouc," had been produced with success. And the pioneer of the dance, the peerless Maraquita, a native Paranoyan, still performed it nightly at the music-hall where she had first broken loose.

The caoutchouc fascinated Roland Bleke. Maraquita fascinated him more. Of all the women to whom he had lost his heart at first sight, Maraquita had made the firmest impression upon him. She was what is sometimes called a fine woman.

She had large, flashing eyes, the physique of a Rugby International forward, and the agility of a cat on hot bricks.

There is a period of about fifty steps somewhere in the middle of the three hundred and fifteen where the patient, abandoning the comparative decorum of the earlier movements, whizzes about till she looks like a salmon-colored whirlwind.

That was the bit that hit Roland.

Night after night he sat in his stage-box, goggling at Maraquita and applauding wildly.

One night an attendant came to his box.

"Excuse me, sir, but are you Mr. Roland Bleke? The Senorita Maraquita wishes to speak to you."

He held open the door of the box. The possibility of refusal did not appear to occur to him. Behind the scenes at that theater, it was generally recognized that when the Peerless One wanted a thing, she got it—quick.

They were alone.

With no protective footlights between himself and her, Roland came to the conclusion that he had made a mistake. It was not that she was any less beautiful at the very close quarters imposed by the limits of the dressing-room; but he felt that in falling in love with her he had undertaken a contract a little too large for one of his quiet, diffident nature. It crossed his mind that the sort of woman he really liked was the rather small, drooping type. Dynamite would not have made Maraquita droop.

For perhaps a minute and a half Maraquita fixed her compelling eyes on his without uttering a word. Then she broke a painful silence with this leading question:

"You love me, hein?"

Roland nodded feebly.

"When men make love to me, I send them away—so."

She waved her hand toward the door, and Roland began to feel almost cheerful again. He was to be dismissed with a caution, after all. The woman had a fine, forgiving nature.

"But not you."

"Not me?"

"No, not you. You are the man I have been waiting for. I read about you in the paper, Senor Bleke. I see your picture in the 'Daily Mirror!' I say to myself, 'What a man!'"

"Those picture-paper photographs always make one look rather weird," mumbled Roland.

"I see you night after night in your box. Poof! I love you."

"Thanks awfully," bleated Roland.

"You would do anything for my sake, hein? I knew you were that kind of man directly I see you. No," she added, as Roland writhed uneasily in his chair, "do not embrace me. Later, yes, but now, no. Not till the Great Day."

What the Great Day might be Roland could not even faintly conjecture. He could only hope that it would also be a remote one.

"And now," said the Senorita, throwing a cloak about her shoulders, "you come away with me to my house. My friends are there awaiting us. They will be glad and proud to meet you."

After his first inspection of the house and the friends, Roland came to the conclusion that he preferred Maraquita's room to her company. The former was large and airy, the latter, with one exception, small and hairy.

The exception Maraquita addressed as Bombito. He was a conspicuous figure. He was one of those out-size, hasty-looking men. One suspected him of carrying lethal weapons.

103

Maraquita presented Roland to the company. The native speech of Paranoya sounded like shorthand, with a blend of Spanish. An expert could evidently squeeze a good deal of it into a minute. Its effect on the company was good. They were manifestly soothed. Even Bombito.

Introductions in detail then took place. This time, for Roland's benefit, Maraquita spoke in English, and he learned that most of those present were marquises. Before him, so he gathered from Maraquita, stood the very flower of Paranoya's aristocracy, driven from their native land by the Infamy of 1905. Roland was too polite to inquire what on earth the Infamy of 1905 might be, but its mention had a marked effect on the company. Some scowled, others uttered deep-throated oaths. Bombito did both. Before supper, to which they presently sat down, was over, however, Roland knew a good deal about Paranoya and its history. The conversation conducted by Maraquita—to a ceaseless bouche pleine accompaniment from her friends—bore exclusively upon the subject.

Paranoya had, it appeared, existed fairly peacefully for centuries under the rule of the Alejandro dynasty. Then, in the reign of Alejandro the Thirteenth, disaffection had begun to spread, culminating in the Infamy of 1905, which, Roland had at last discovered, was nothing less than the abolition of the monarchy and the installation of a republic.

Since 1905 the one thing for which they had lived, besides the caoutchouc, was to see the monarchy restored and their beloved Alejandro the Thirteenth back on his throne. Their efforts toward this end had been untiring, and were at last showing signs of bearing fruit. Paranoya, Maraquita assured Roland, was honeycombed with intrigue. The army was disaffected, the people anxious for a return to the old order of things.

A more propitious moment for striking the decisive blow was never likely to arrive. The question was purely one of funds.

At the mention of the word "funds," Roland, who had become thoroughly bored with the lecture on Paranoyan history, sat up and took notice. He had an instinctive feeling that he was about to be called upon for a subscription to the cause of the distressful country's freedom. Especially by Bombito.

He was right. A moment later Maraquita began to make a speech.

She spoke in Paranoyan, and Roland could not follow her, but he gathered that it somehow had reference to himself.

As, at the end of it, the entire company rose to their feet and extended their glasses toward him with a mighty shout, he assumed that Maraquita had been proposing his health.

"They say 'To the liberator of Paranoya!'" kindly translated the Peerless One. "You must excuse," said Maraquita tolerantly, as a bevy of patriots surrounded Roland and kissed him on the cheek. "They are so grateful to the savior of our country. I myself would kiss you, were it not that I have sworn that no man's lips shall touch mine till the royal standard floats once more above the palace of Paranoya. But that will be soon, very soon," she went on. "With you on our side we can not fail."

What did the woman mean? Roland asked himself wildly. Did she labor under the distressing delusion that he proposed to shed his blood on behalf of a deposed monarch to whom he had never been introduced?

Maraquita's next remarks made the matter clear.

"I have told them," she said, "that you love me, that you are willing to risk everything for my sake. I have promised them that you, the rich Senor Bleke, will supply the funds for the revolution. Once more, comrades. To the Savior of Paranoya!"

Roland tried his hardest to catch the infection of this patriotic enthusiasm, but somehow he could not do it. Base, sordid, mercenary speculations would intrude themselves. About how much was a good, well-furnished revolution likely to cost? As delicately as he could, he put the question to Maraquita.

She said, "Poof! The cost? La, la!" Which was all very well, but hardly satisfactory as a business chat. However, that was all Roland could get out of her.

The next few days passed for Roland in a sort of dream. It was the kind of dream which it is not easy to distinguish from a nightmare.

Maraquita's reticence at the supper-party on the subject of details connected with the financial side of revolutions entirely disappeared. She now talked nothing but figures, and from the confused mass which she presented to him Roland was able to gather that, in financing the restoration of royalty in Paranoya, he would indeed be risking everything for her sake.

In the matter of revolutions Maraquita was no niggard. She knew how the thing should be done—well, or not at all. There would be so much for rifles, machine-guns, and what not: and there would be so much for the expense of smuggling them into the country. Then there would be so much to be laid out in corrupting the republican army. Roland brightened a little when they came to this item. As the standing army of Paranoya amounted to twenty thousand men, and as it seemed possible to corrupt it thoroughly at a cost of about thirty shillings a head, the obvious course, to Roland's way of thinking was to concentrate on this side of the question and avoid unnecessary bloodshed.

It appeared, however, that Maraquita did not want to avoid bloodshed, that she rather liked bloodshed, that the leaders of the revolution would be disappointed if there were no bloodshed. Especially Bombito. Unless, she pointed out, there was a certain amount of carnage, looting, and so on, the revolution would not achieve a popular success. True, the beloved Alejandro might be restored; but he would sit upon a throne that was insecure, unless the coronation festivities took a bloodthirsty turn. By all means, said Maraquita, corrupt the army, but not at the risk of making the affair tame and unpopular. Paranoya was an emotional country, and liked its revolutions with a bit of zip to them.

It was about ten days after he had definitely cast in his lot with the revolutionary party that Roland was made aware that these things were a little more complex than he had imagined. He had reconciled himself to the financial outlay. It had been difficult, but he had done it. That his person as well as his purse would be placed in peril he had not foreseen.

The fact was borne in upon him at the end of the second week by the arrival of the deputation.

It blew in from the street just as he was enjoying his after-dinner cigar.

It consisted of three men, one long and suave, the other two short, stout, and silent. They all had the sallow complexion and undue hairiness which he had come by this time to associate with the native of Paranoya.

For a moment he mistook them for a drove of exiled noblemen whom he had not had the pleasure of meeting at the supper-party; and he waited resignedly for them to make night hideous with the royal anthem. He poised himself on his toes, the more readily to spring aside if they should try to kiss him on the cheek.

"Mr. Bleke?" said the long man.

His companions drifted toward the cigar-box which stood open on the table, and looked at it wistfully.

"Long live the monarchy," said Roland wearily. He had gathered in the course of his dealings with the exiled ones that this remark generally went well.

On the present occasion it elicited no outburst of cheering. On the contrary, the long man frowned, and his two companions helped themselves to a handful of cigars apiece with a marked moodiness.

106

"Death to the monarchy," corrected the long man coldly. "And," he added with a wealth of meaning in his voice, "to all who meddle in the affairs of our beloved country and seek to do it harm."

"I don't know what you mean," said Roland.

"Yes, Senor Bleke, you do know what I mean. I mean that you will be well advised to abandon the schemes which you are hatching with the malcontents who would do my beloved land an injury."

The conversation was growing awkward. Roland had got so into the habit of taking it for granted that every Paranoyan he met must of necessity be a devotee of the beloved Alejandro that it came as a shock to him to realize that there were those who objected to his restoration to the throne. Till now he had looked on the enemy as something in the abstract. It had not struck him that the people for whose correction he was buying all these rifles and machine-guns were individuals with a lively distaste for having their blood shed.

"Senor Bleke," resumed the speaker, frowning at one of his companions whose hand was hovering above the bottle of liqueur brandy, "you are a man of sense. You know what is safe and what is not safe. Believe me, this scheme of yours is not safe. You have been led away, but there is still time to withdraw. Do so, and all is well. Do not so, and your blood be upon your own head."

"My blood!" gasped Roland.

The speaker bowed.

"That is all," he said. "We merely came to give the warning. Ah, Senor Bleke, do not be rash. You think that here, in this great London of yours, you are safe. You look at the policeman upon the corner of the road, and you say to yourself 'I am safe.' Believe me, not at all so is it, but much the opposite. We have ways by which it is of no account the policeman on the corner of the road. That is all, Senor Bleke. We wish you a good night."

The deputation withdrew.

Maraquita, informed of the incident, snapped her fingers, and said "Poof!" It sometimes struck Roland that she would be more real help in a difficult situation if she could get out of the habit of saying "Poof!"

"It is nothing," she said.

"No?" said Roland.

"We easily out-trick them, isn't it? You make a will leaving your money to the Cause, and then where are they, hein?"

It was one way of looking at it, but it brought little balm to Roland. He said so. Maraquita scanned his face keenly.

107

"You are not weakening, Roland?" she said. "You would not betray us now?"

"Well, of course, I don't know about betraying, you know, but still——. What I mean is——"

Maraquita's eyes seemed to shoot forth two flames.

"Take care," she cried. "With me it is nothing, for I know that your heart is with Paranoya. But, if the others once had cause to suspect that your resolve was failing—ah! If Bombito——"

Roland took her point. He had forgotten Bombito for the moment.

"For goodness' sake," he said hastily, "don't go saying anything to Bombito to give him the idea that I'm trying to back out. Of course you can rely on me, and all that. That's all right."

Maraquita's gaze softened. She raised her glass—they were lunching at the time—and put it to her lips.

"To the Savior of Paranoya!" she said.

"Beware!" whispered a voice in Roland's ear.

He turned with a start. A waiter was standing behind him, a small, dark, hairy man. He was looking into the middle distance with the abstracted air which waiters cultivate.

Roland stared at him, but he did not move.

That evening, returning to his flat, Roland was paralyzed by the sight of the word "Beware" scrawled across the mirror in his bedroom. It had apparently been done with a diamond. He rang the bell.

"Sir?" said the competent valet. ("Competent valets are in attendance at each of these flats."—Advt.)

"Has any one been here since I left?"

"Yes, sir. A foreign-looking gentleman called. He said he knew you, sir. I showed him into your room."

The same night, well on in the small hours, the telephone rang. Roland dragged himself out of bed.

"Hullo?"

"Is that Senor Bleke?"

"Yes. What is it?"

"Beware!"

Things were becoming intolerable. Roland had a certain amount of nerve, but not enough to enable him to bear up against this sinister persecution. Yet what could he do? Suppose he did beware to the extent of withdrawing his support from the royalist movement, what then? Bombito. If ever there was a toad under the harrow, he was that toad. And all because a perfectly respectful admiration for the caoutchouc had led him to occupy a stage-box several nights in succession at the theater where the peerless Maraquita tied herself into knots.

There was an air of unusual excitement in Maraquita's manner at their next meeting.

"We have been in communication with Him," she whispered. "He will receive you. He will give an audience to the Savior of Paranoya."

"Eh? Who will?"

"Our beloved Alejandro. He wishes to see his faithful servant. We are to go to him at once."

"Where?"

"At his own house. He will receive you in person."

Such was the quality of the emotions through which he had been passing of late, that Roland felt but a faint interest at the prospect of meeting face to face a genuine—if exiled—monarch. The thought did flit through his mind that they would sit up a bit in old Fineberg's office if they could hear of it, but it brought him little consolation.

The cab drew up at a gloomy-looking house in a fashionable square. Roland rang the door-bell. There seemed a certain element of the prosaic in the action. He wondered what he should say to the butler.

There was, however, no need for words. The door opened, and they were ushered in without parley. A butler and two footmen showed them into a luxuriously furnished anteroom. Roland entered with two thoughts running in his mind. The first was that the beloved Alejandro had got an uncommonly snug crib; the second that this was exactly like going to see the dentist.

Presently the squad of retainers returned, the butler leading.

"His Majesty will receive Mr. Bleke."

Roland followed him with tottering knees.

His Majesty, King Alejandro the Thirteenth, on the retired list, was a genial-looking man of middle age, comfortably stout about the middle and a little bald as to the forehead. He might have been a prosperous stock-broker. Roland felt more at his ease at the very sight of him.

"Sit down, Mr. Bleke," said His Majesty, as the door closed. "I have been wanting to see you for some time."

Roland had nothing to say. He was regaining his composure, but he had a long way to go yet before he could feel thoroughly at home.

King Alejandro produced a cigaret-case, and offered it to

Roland, who shook his head speechlessly. The King lit a cigaret and smoked thoughtfully for a while.

"You know, Mr. Bleke," he said at last, "this must stop. It really must. I mean your devoted efforts on my behalf."

Roland gaped at him.

"You are a very young man. I had expected to see some one much older. Your youth gives me the impression that you have gone into this affair from a spirit of adventure. I can assure you that you have nothing to gain commercially by interfering with my late kingdom. I hope, before we part, that I can persuade you to abandon your idea of financing this movement to restore me to the throne.

"I don't understand—er—your majesty."

"I will explain. Please treat what I shall say as strictly confidential. You must know, Mr. Bleke, that these attempts to re-establish me as a reigning monarch in Paranoya are, frankly, the curse of an otherwise very pleasant existence. You look surprized? My dear sir, do you know Paranoya? Have you ever been there? Have you the remotest idea what sort of life a King of Paranoya leads? I have tried it, and I can assure you that a coal-heaver is happy by comparison. In the first place, the climate of the country is abominable. I always had a cold in the head. Secondly, there is a small but energetic section of the populace whose sole recreation it seems to be to use their monarch as a target for bombs. They are not very good bombs, it is true, but one in, say, ten explodes, and even an occasional bomb is unpleasant if you are the target.

"Finally, I am much too fond of your delightful country to wish to leave it. I was educated in England—I am a Magdalene College man—and I have the greatest horror of ever being compelled to leave it. My present life suits me exactly. That is all I wished to say, Mr. Bleke. For both our sakes, for the sake of my comfort and your purse, abandon this scheme of yours."

Roland walked home thoughtfully. Maraquita had left the royal residence long before he had finished the whisky-and-soda which the genial monarch had pressed upon him. As he walked, the futility of his situation came home to him more and more. Whatever he did, he was bound to displease somebody; and these Paranoyans were so confoundedly impulsive when they were vexed.

For two days he avoided Maraquita. On the third, with something of the instinct which draws the murderer to the spot where he has buried the body, he called at her house.

She was not present, but otherwise there was a full gathering.

There were the marquises; there were the counts; there was Bombito.

He looked unhappily round the crowd.

Somebody gave him a glass of champagne. He raised it.

"To the revolution," he said mechanically.

There was a silence—it seemed to Roland an awkward silence. As if he had said something improper, the marquises and counts began to drift from the room, till only Bombito was left. Roland regarded him with some apprehension. He was looking larger and more unusual than ever.

But to-night, apparently, Bombito was in genial mood. He came forward and slapped Roland on the shoulder. And then the remarkable fact came to light that Bombito spoke English, or a sort of English.

"My old chap," he said. "I would have a speech with you."

He slapped Roland again on the shoulder.

"The others they say, 'Break it with Senor Bleke gently.' Maraquita say 'Break it with Senor Bleke gently.' So I break it with you gently."

He dealt Roland a third stupendous punch. Whatever was to be broken gently, it was plain to Roland that it was not himself. And suddenly there came to him a sort of intuition that told him that Bombito was nervous.

"After all you have done for us, Senor Bleke, we shall seem to you ungrateful bounders, but what is it? Yes? No? I shouldn't wonder, perhaps. The whole fact is that there has been political crisis in Paranoya. Upset. Apple-cart. Yes? You follow? No? The Ministry have been—what do you say?—put through it. Expelled. Broken up. No more ministry. New ministry wanted. To conciliate royalist party, that is the cry. So deputation of leading persons, mighty good chaps, prominent merchants and that sort of bounder, call upon us. They offer me to be President. See? No? Yes? That's right. I am ambitious blighter, Senor Bleke. What about it, no? I accept. I am new President of Paranoya. So no need for your kind assistance. Royalist revolution up the spout. No more royalist revolution."

The wave of relief which swept over Roland ebbed sufficiently after an interval to enable him to think of some one but himself. He was not fond of Maraquita, but he had a tender heart, and this, he felt, would kill the poor girl.

"But Maraquita——?"

"That's all right, splendid old chap. No need to worry about Maraquita, stout old boy. Where the husband goes, so does the wife go. As you say, whither thou goes will I follow. No?"

"But I don't understand. Maraquita is not your wife?"

"Why, certainly, good old heart. What else?"

"Have you been married to her all the time?"

"Why, certainly, good, dear boy."

The room swam before Roland's eyes. There was no room in his mind for meditations on the perfidy of woman. He groped forward and found Bombito's hand.

"By Jove," he said thickly, as he wrung it again and again, "I knew you were a good sort the first time I saw you. Have a drink or something. Have a cigar or something. Have something, anyway, and sit down and tell me all about it."

THE EPISODE OF THE HIRED PAST

Final Story of the Series [First published in Pictorial Review, October 1916]

"What do you mean—you can't marry him after all? After all what? Why can't you marry him? You are perfectly childish."

Lord Evenwood's gentle voice, which had in its time lulled the House of Peers to slumber more often than any voice ever heard in the Gilded Chamber, had in it a note of unwonted, but quite justifiable, irritation. If there was one thing more than another that Lord Evenwood disliked, it was any interference with arrangements already made.

"The man," he continued, "is not unsightly. The man is not conspicuously vulgar. The man does not eat peas with his knife. The man pronounces his aitches with meticulous care and accuracy. The man, moreover, is worth rather more than a quarter of a million pounds. I repeat, you are childish!"

"Yes, I know he's a very decent little chap, Father," said Lady Eva. "It's not that at all."

"I should be gratified, then, to hear what, in your opinion, it is."

"Well, do you think I could be happy with him?"

Lady Kimbuck gave tongue. She was Lord Evenwood's sister. She spent a very happy widowhood interfering in the affairs of the various branches of her family.

"We're not asking you to be happy. You have such odd ideas of happiness. Your idea of happiness is to be married to your cousin Gerry, whose only visible means of support, so far as I can gather, is the four hundred a year which he draws as a member for a constituency which has every intention of throwing him out at the next election."

Lady Eva blushed. Lady Kimbuck's faculty for nosing out the secrets of her family had made her justly disliked from the Hebrides to Southern Cornwall.

113

"Young O'Rion is not to be thought of," said Lord Evenwood firmly. "Not for an instant. Apart from anything else, his politics are all wrong. Moreover, you are engaged to this Mr. Bleke. It is a sacred responsibility not lightly to be evaded. You can not pledge your word one day to enter upon the most solemn contract known to—ah—the civilized world, and break it the next. It is not fair to the man. It is not fair to me. You know that all I live for is to see you comfortably settled. If I could myself do anything for you, the matter would be different. But these abominable land-taxes and Blowick—especially Blowick—no, no, it's out of the question. You will be very sorry if you do anything foolish. I can assure you that Roland Blekes are not to be found—ah—on every bush. Men are extremely shy of marrying nowadays."

"Especially," said Lady Kimbuck, "into a family like ours. What with Blowick's scandal, and that shocking business of your grandfather and the circus-woman, to say nothing of your poor father's trouble in '85——"

"Thank you, Sophia," interrupted Lord Evenwood, hurriedly. "It is unnecessary to go into all that now. Suffice it that there are adequate reasons, apart from all moral obligations, why Eva should not break her word to Mr. Bleke."

Lady Kimbuck's encyclopedic grip of the family annals was a source of the utmost discomfort to her relatives. It was known that more than one firm of publishers had made her tempting offers for her reminiscences, and the family looked on like nervous spectators at a battle while Cupidity fought its ceaseless fight with Laziness; for the Evenwood family had at various times and in various ways stimulated the circulation of the evening papers. Most of them were living down something, and it was Lady Kimbuck's habit, when thwarted in her lightest whim, to retire to her boudoir and announce that she was not to be disturbed as she was at last making a start on her book. Abject surrender followed on the instant.

At this point in the discussion she folded up her crochet-work, and rose.

"It is absolutely necessary for you, my dear, to make a good match, or you will all be ruined. I, of course, can always support my declining years with literary work, but——"

Lady Eva groaned. Against this last argument there was no appeal.

Lady Kimbuck patted her affectionately on the shoulder.

"There, run along now," she said. "I daresay you've got a headache or something that made you say a lot of foolish things you didn't mean. Go down to the drawing-room. I expect Mr. Bleke is waiting there to say goodnight to you. I am sure he must be getting quite impatient."

Down in the drawing-room, Roland Bleke was hoping against hope that Lady Eva's prolonged absence might be due to the fact that she had gone to bed with a headache, and that he might escape the nightly interview which he so dreaded.

Reviewing his career, as he sat there, Roland came to the conclusion that women had the knack of affecting him with a form of temporary insanity. They temporarily changed his whole nature. They made him feel for a brief while that he was a dashing young man capable of the highest flights of love. It was only later that the reaction came and he realized that he was nothing of the sort.

At heart he was afraid of women, and in the entire list of the women of whom he had been afraid, he could not find one who had terrified him so much as Lady Eva Blyton.

Other women—notably Maraquita, now happily helping to direct the destinies of Paranoya—had frightened him by their individuality. Lady Eva frightened him both by her individuality and the atmosphere of aristocratic exclusiveness which she conveyed. He had no idea whatever of what was the proper procedure for a man engaged to the daughter of an earl. Daughters of earls had been to him till now mere names in the society columns of the morning paper. The very rules of the game were beyond him. He felt like a confirmed Association footballer suddenly called upon to play in an International Rugby match.

All along, from the very moment when—to his unbounded astonishment—she had accepted him, he had known that he was making a mistake; but he never realized it with such painful clearness as he did this evening. He was filled with a sort of blind terror. He cursed the fate which had taken him to the Charity-Bazaar at which he had first come under the notice of Lady Kimbuck. The fatuous snobbishness which had made him leap at her invitation to spend a few days at Evenwood Towers he regretted; but for that he blamed himself less. Further acquaintance with Lady Kimbuck had convinced him that if she had wanted him, she would have got him somehow, whether he had accepted or refused.

What he really blamed himself for was his mad proposal. There had been no need for it. True, Lady Eva had created a riot of burning emotions in his breast from the moment they met; but he should have had the sense to realize that she was not the right mate for him, even tho he might have a quarter of a million tucked away in gilt-edged securities. Their lives could not possibly mix. He was a commonplace young man with a fondness for the pleasures of the people. He liked cheap papers, picture-palaces, and Association football. Merely to think of Association football in connection with her was enough to make the folly of his conduct clear. He ought to have been content to worship her from afar as some inaccessible goddess.

A light step outside the door made his heart stop beating.

"I've just looked in to say good night, Mr.—er—Roland," she said, holding out her hand. "Do excuse me. I've got such a headache."

"Oh, yes, rather; I'm awfully sorry."

If there was one person in the world Roland despised and hated at that moment, it was himself.

"Are you going out with the guns to-morrow?" asked Lady Eva languidly.

"Oh, yes, rather! I mean, no. I'm afraid I don't shoot."

The back of his neck began to glow. He had no illusions about himself. He was the biggest ass in Christendom.

"Perhaps you'd like to play a round of golf, then?"

"Oh, yes, rather! I mean, no." There it was again, that awful phrase. He was certain he had not intended to utter it. She must be thinking him a perfect lunatic. "I don't play golf."

They stood looking at each other for a moment. It seemed to Roland that her gaze was partly contemptuous, partly pitying. He longed to tell her that, tho she had happened to pick on his weak points in the realm of sport, there were things he could do. An insane desire came upon him to babble about his school football team. Should he ask her to feel his quite respectable biceps? No.

"Never mind," she said, kindly. "I daresay we shall think of something to amuse you."

She held out her hand again. He took it in his for the briefest possible instant, painfully conscious the while that his own hand was clammy from the emotion through which he had been passing.

"Good night."

"Good night."

Thank Heaven, she was gone. That let him out for another twelve hours at least.

A quarter of an hour later found Roland still sitting, where she had left him, his head in his hands. The groan of an overwrought soul escaped him.

"I can't do it!"

He sprang to his feet.

"I won't do it."

A smooth voice from behind him spoke.

"I think you are quite right, sir—if I may make the remark."

Roland had hardly ever been so startled in his life. In the first place, he was not aware of having uttered his thoughts aloud; in the second, he had imagined that he was alone in the room. And so, a moment before, he had been.

But the owner of the voice possessed, among other qualities, the cat-like faculty of entering a room perfectly noiselessly—a fact which had won for him, in the course of a long career in the service of the best families, the flattering position of star witness in a number of England's raciest divorce-cases.

Mr. Teal, the butler—for it was no less a celebrity who had broken in on Roland's reverie—was a long, thin man of a somewhat priestly cast of countenance. He lacked that air of reproving hauteur which many butlers possess, and it was for this reason that Roland had felt drawn to him during the black days of his stay at Evenwood Towers. Teal had been uncommonly nice to him on the whole. He had seemed to Roland, stricken by interviews with his host and Lady Kimbuck, the only human thing in the place.

He liked Teal. On the other hand, Teal was certainly taking a liberty. He could, if he so pleased, tell Teal to go to the deuce. Technically, he had the right to freeze Teal with a look.

He did neither of these things. He was feeling very lonely and very forlorn in a strange and depressing world, and Teal's voice and manner were soothing.

"Hearing you speak, and seeing nobody else in the room," went on the butler, "I thought for a moment that you were addressing me."

This was not true, and Roland knew it was not true. Instinct told him that Teal knew that he knew it was not true; but he did not press the point.

"What do you mean—you think I am quite right?" he said. "You don't know what I was thinking about."

Teal smiled indulgently.

"On the contrary, sir. A child could have guessed it. You have just come to the decision—in my opinion a thoroughly sensible one—that your engagement to her ladyship can not be allowed to go on. You are quite right, sir. It won't do."

Personal magnetism covers a multitude of sins. Roland was perfectly well aware that he ought not to be standing here chatting over his and Lady Eva's intimate affairs with a butler; but such was Teal's magnetism that he was quite unable to do the right thing and

117

tell him to mind his own business. "Teal, you forget yourself!" would have covered the situation. Roland, however, was physically incapable of saying "Teal, you forget yourself!" The bird knows all the time that he ought not to stand talking to the snake, but he is incapable of ending the conversation. Roland was conscious of a momentary wish that he was the sort of man who could tell butlers that they forgot themselves. But then that sort of man would never be in this sort of trouble. The "Teal, you forget yourself" type of man would be a first-class shot, a plus golfer, and would certainly consider himself extremely lucky to be engaged to Lady Eva.

"The question is," went on Mr. Teal, "how are we to break it off?"

Roland felt that, as he had sinned against all the decencies in allowing the butler to discuss his affairs with him, he might just as well go the whole hog and allow the discussion to run its course. And it was an undeniable relief to talk about the infernal thing to some one.

He nodded gloomily, and committed himself. Teal resumed his remarks with the gusto of a fellow-conspirator.

"It's not an easy thing to do gracefully, sir, believe me, it isn't. And it's got to be done gracefully, or not at all. You can't go to her ladyship and say 'It's all off, and so am I,' and catch the next train for London. The rupture must be of her ladyship's making. If some fact, some disgraceful information concerning you were to come to her ladyship's ears, that would be a simple way out of the difficulty."

He eyed Roland meditatively.

"If, for instance, you had ever been in jail, sir?"

"Well, I haven't."

"No offense intended, sir, I'm sure. I merely remembered that you had made a great deal of money very quickly. My experience of gentlemen who have made a great deal of money very quickly is that they have generally done their bit of time. But, of course, if you——. Let me think. Do you drink, sir?"

"No."

Mr. Teal sighed. Roland could not help feeling that he was disappointing the old man a good deal.

"You do not, I suppose, chance to have a past?" asked Mr. Teal, not very hopefully. "I use the word in its technical sense. A deserted wife? Some poor creature you have treated shamefully?"

At the risk of sinking still further in the butler's esteem, Roland was compelled to answer in the negative.

"I was afraid not," said Mr. Teal, shaking his head. "Thinking it all over yesterday, I said to myself, 'I'm afraid he wouldn't have

118

one.' You don't look like the sort of gentleman who had done much with his time."

"Thinking it over?"

"Not on your account, sir," explained Mr. Teal. "On the family's. I disapproved of this match from the first. A man who has served a family as long as I have had the honor of serving his lordship's, comes to entertain a high regard for the family prestige. And, with no offense to yourself, sir, this would not have done."

"Well, it looks as if it would have to do," said Roland, gloomily. "I can't see any way out of it."

"I can, sir. My niece at Aldershot."

Mr. Teal wagged his head at him with a kind of priestly archness.

"You can not have forgotten my niece at Aldershot?"

Roland stared at him dumbly. It was like a line out of a melodrama. He feared, first for his own, then for the butler's sanity. The latter was smiling gently, as one who sees light in a difficult situation.

"I've never been at Aldershot in my life."

"For our purposes you have, sir. But I'm afraid I am puzzling you. Let me explain. I've got a niece over at Aldershot who isn't much good. She's not very particular. I am sure she would do it for a consideration."

"Do what?"

"Be your 'Past,' sir. I don't mind telling you that as a 'Past' she's had some experience; looks the part, too. She's a barmaid, and you would guess it the first time you saw her. Dyed yellow hair, sir," he went on with enthusiasm, "done all frizzy. Just the sort of young person that a young gentleman like yourself would have had a 'past' with. You couldn't find a better if you tried for a twelvemonth."

"But, I say——!"

"I suppose a hundred wouldn't hurt you?"

"Well, no, I suppose not, but——"

"Then put the whole thing in my hands, sir. I'll ask leave off to-morrow and pop over and see her. I'll arrange for her to come here the day after to see you. Leave it all to me. To-night you must write the letters."

"Letters?"

"Naturally, there would be letters, sir. It is an inseparable feature of these cases."

"Do you mean that I have got to write to her? But I shouldn't know what to say. I've never seen her."

"That will be quite all right, sir, if you place yourself in my hands. I will come to your room after everybody's gone to bed, and help you write those letters. You have some note-paper with your own address on it? Then it will all be perfectly simple."

When, some hours later, he read over the ten or twelve exceedingly passionate epistles which, with the butler's assistance, he had succeeded in writing to Miss Maud Chilvers, Roland came to the conclusion that there must have been a time when Mr. Teal was a good deal less respectable than he appeared to be at present. Byronic was the only adjective applicable to his collaborator's style of amatory composition. In every letter there were passages against which Roland had felt compelled to make a modest protest.

"'A thousand kisses on your lovely rosebud of a mouth.' Don't you think that is a little too warmly colored? And 'I am languishing for the pressure of your ivory arms about my neck and the sweep of your silken hair against my cheek!' What I mean is—well, what about it, you know?"

"The phrases," said Mr. Teal, not without a touch of displeasure, "to which you take exception, are taken bodily from correspondence (which I happened to have the advantage of perusing) addressed by the late Lord Evenwood to Animalcula, Queen of the High Wire at Astley's Circus. His lordship, I may add, was considered an authority in these matters."

Roland criticized no more. He handed over the letters, which, at Mr. Teal's direction, he had headed with various dates covering roughly a period of about two months antecedent to his arrival at the Towers.

"That," Mr. Teal explained, "will make your conduct definitely unpardonable. With this woman's kisses hot upon your lips,"—Mr. Teal was still slightly aglow with the fire of inspiration—"you have the effrontery to come here and offer yourself to her ladyship."

With Roland's timid suggestion that it was perhaps a mistake to overdo the atmosphere, the butler found himself unable to agree.

"You can't make yourself out too bad. If you don't pitch it hot and strong, her ladyship might quite likely forgive you. Then where would you be?"

Miss Maud Chilvers, of Aldershot, burst into Roland's life like one of the shells of her native heath two days later at about five in the afternoon.

It was an entrance of which any stage-manager might have been proud of having arranged. The lighting, the grouping, the lead-up—all were perfect. The family had just finished tea in the long drawing-room. Lady Kimbuck was crocheting, Lord Evenwood dozing, Lady Eva reading, and Roland thinking. A peaceful scene.

A soft, rippling murmur, scarcely to be reckoned a snore, had just proceeded from Lord Evenwood's parted lips, when the door opened, and Teal announced, "Miss Chilvers."

Roland stiffened in his chair. Now that the ghastly moment had come, he felt too petrified with fear even to act the little part in which he had been diligently rehearsed by the obliging Mr. Teal. He simply sat and did nothing.

It was speedily made clear to him that Miss Chilvers would do all the actual doing that was necessary. The butler had drawn no false picture of her personal appearance. Dyed yellow hair done all frizzy was but one fact of her many-sided impossibilities. In the serene surroundings of the long drawing-room, she looked more unspeakably "not much good" than Roland had ever imagined her. With such a leading lady, his drama could not fail of success. He should have been pleased; he was merely appalled. The thing might have a happy ending, but while it lasted it was going to be terrible.

She had a flatteringly attentive reception. Nobody failed to notice her. Lord Evenwood woke with a start, and stared at her as if she had been some ghost from his trouble of '85. Lady Eva's face expressed sheer amazement. Lady Kimbuck, laying down her crochet-work, took one look at the apparition, and instantly decided that one of her numerous erring relatives had been at it again. Of all the persons in the room, she was possibly the only one completely cheerful. She was used to these situations and enjoyed them. Her mind, roaming into the past, recalled the night when her cousin Warminster had been pinked by a stiletto in his own drawing-room by a lady from South America. Happy days, happy days.

Lord Evenwood had, by this time, come to the conclusion that the festive Blowick must be responsible for this visitation. He rose with dignity.

"To what are we——?" he began.

Miss Chilvers, resolute young woman, had no intention of standing there while other people talked. She shook her gleaming head and burst into speech.

"Oh, yes, I know I've no right to be coming walking in here among a lot of perfect strangers at their teas, but what I say is, 'Right's right and wrong's wrong all the world over,' and I may be poor, but I have my feelings. No, thank you, I won't sit down. I've not come for the weekend. I've come to say a few words, and when I've said them I'll go, and not before. A lady friend of mine happened to be reading her Daily Sketch the other day, and she said 'Hullo! hullo!' and passed it on to me with her thumb on a picture which had under it that it was Lady Eva Blyton who was engaged to

121

be married to Mr. Roland Bleke. And when I read that, I said 'Hullo! hullo!' too, I give you my word. And not being able to travel at once, owing to being prostrated with the shock, I came along to-day, just to have a look at Mr. Roland Blooming Bleke, and ask him if he's forgotten that he happens to be engaged to me. That's all. I know it's the sort of thing that might slip any gentleman's mind, but I thought it might be worth mentioning. So now!"

Roland, perspiring in the shadows at the far end of the room, felt that Miss Chilvers was overdoing it. There was no earthly need for all this sort of thing. Just a simple announcement of the engagement would have been quite sufficient. It was too obvious to him that his ally was thoroughly enjoying herself. She had the center of the stage, and did not intend lightly to relinquish it.

"My good girl," said Lady Kimbuck, "talk less and prove more. When did Mr. Bleke promise to marry you?"

"Oh, it's all right. I'm not expecting you to believe my word. I've got all the proofs you'll want. Here's his letters."

Lady Kimbuck's eyes gleamed. She took the package eagerly. She never lost an opportunity of reading compromising letters. She enjoyed them as literature, and there was never any knowing when they might come in useful.

"Roland," said Lady Eva, quietly, "haven't you anything to contribute to this conversation?"

Miss Chilvers clutched at her bodice. Cinema palaces were a passion with her, and she was up in the correct business.

"Is he here? In this room?"

Roland slunk from the shadows.

"Mr. Bleke," said Lord Evenwood, sternly, "who is this woman?"

Roland uttered a kind of strangled cough.

"Are these letters in your handwriting?" asked Lady Kimbuck, almost cordially. She had seldom read better compromising letters in her life, and she was agreeably surprized that one whom she had always imagined a colorless stick should have been capable of them.

Roland nodded.

"Well, it's lucky you're rich," said Lady Kimbuck philosophically. "What are you asking for these?" she enquired of Miss Chilvers.

"Exactly," said Lord Evenwood, relieved. "Precisely. Your sterling common sense is admirable, Sophia. You place the whole matter at once on a businesslike footing."

"Do you imagine for a moment——?" began Miss Chilvers slowly.

"Yes," said Lady Kimbuck. "How much?"

Miss Chilvers sobbed.

"If I have lost him for ever——"

Lady Eva rose.

"But you haven't," she said pleasantly. "I wouldn't dream of standing in your way." She drew a ring from her finger, placed it on the table, and walked to the door. "I am not engaged to Mr. Bleke," she said, as she reached it.

Roland never knew quite how he had got away from The Towers. He had confused memories in which the principals of the drawing-room scene figured in various ways, all unpleasant. It was a portion of his life on which he did not care to dwell. Safely back in his flat, however, he gradually recovered his normal spirits. Indeed, now that the tumult and the shouting had, so to speak, died, and he was free to take a broad view of his position, he felt distinctly happier than usual. That Lady Kimbuck had passed for ever from his life was enough in itself to make for gaiety.

He was humming blithely one morning as he opened his letters; outside the sky was blue and the sun shining. It was good to be alive. He opened the first letter. The sky was still blue, the sun still shining.

> "Dear Sir," (it ran).
>
> "We have been instructed by our client, Miss Maud Chilvers, of the Goat and Compasses, Aldershot, to institute proceedings against you for Breach of Promise of Marriage. In the event of your being desirous to avoid the expense and publicity of litigation, we are instructed to say that Miss Chilvers would be prepared to accept the sum of ten thousand pounds in settlement of her claim against you. We would further add that in support of her case our client has in her possession a number of letters written by yourself to her, all of which bear strong prima facie evidence of the alleged promise to marry: and she will be able in addition to call as witnesses in support of her case the Earl of Evenwood, Lady Kimbuck, and Lady Eva Blyton, in whose presence, at a recent date, you acknowledged that you had promised to marry our client.
>
> "Trusting that we hear from you in the course of post.
>   We are, dear Sir,
>   Yours faithfully,
>   Harrison, Harrison, Harrison, & Harrison."

www.ingramcontent.com/pod-product-compliance
Lightning Source LLC
Chambersburg PA
CBHW011516170626
46810CB00009B/3387